Blue
Heron

BY *AVI*

Bradbury Press/**New York**

Maxwell Macmillan Canada/Toronto
Maxwell Macmillan International
New York/Oxford/Singapore/Sydney

Bradbury Press
Macmillan Publishing Company
866 Third Avenue
New York, NY 10022

Maxwell Macmillan Canada, Inc.
1200 Eglinton Avenue East
Suite 200
Don Mills, Ontario M3C 3N1

Macmillan Publishing Company is part of the Maxwell Communication Group of Companies.

First edition
Printed and bound in the United States of America

10 9 8 7 6 5 4 3 2 1

The text of this book is set in Garamond #3.

Library of Congress Cataloging-in-Publication Data
Avi, date–
  Blue heron / by Avi.
     p.   cm.
  Summary: While spending the month of August on the Massachusetts shore with her father, stepmother, and their new baby, almost thirteen-year-old Maggie finds beauty in and draws strength from a great blue heron, even as the family around her unravels.
  ISBN 0-02-707751-9
  {1. Family problems—Fiction.   2. Herons—Fiction.   3. Friendship—Fiction.}   I. Title.
  PZ7.A953B1   1992
  {Fic}—dc20   91-4308

AR/BL: 4.0   Pts: 5.0
J
AVI
Blue heron

S

DATE DUE

32824

Blue Heron

For My Father

_____

CHAPTER

1

What—Margaret Lavchek asked herself—
was magic really for? As far as she was concerned, people did not understand magic
properly. Magic was *not* to change things.
No, magic was a way of keeping things the
way they were. So as Maggie—the name she liked people to use—put aside *Ancient Tales of Magic*, she made
the wish that nothing about her father had changed.

Considering Maggie's age—she was almost thirteen—
she was both tall and strong. That, and her frank brown
eyes, plus a willing smile, added to her outwardly assured
manner. But as the plane moved into its steady descent,
it was with feelings of nervousness and a frowning face
that Maggie looked out the porthole. She was trying to
compare what she saw below with the map her father
had sent her.

Was that the village of Westport she was seeing? If it was Westport, she should be over the Westport River with its two branches meeting like the letter Y and flowing into the sea. Sure enough, she could make it out. That made her certain she was looking right down at Sawdy Pond, where her father and his wife had taken a cottage for the month of August.

Between visits—Christmas and August—Maggie spoke to her dad at least twice a week. And she got along with Joanna, his wife of two years. Summer visits with him, now with them—they lived in Boston—had always been a frenzy of doing things, going places, movies, museums, concerts, one long party.

But below, in that same lakeside cottage, was her new half sister, Linda, four months old. Maggie was not sure how she felt about Linda, or how Linda's coming into the family was going to change things. Maggie scolded herself for being so apprehensive. But then, since leaving her home in Seattle, Washington, that morning, she had traveled for seven hours. She was tired and wanted to be there.

From her jeans pocket Maggie pulled out an egg-shaped, multisided glass crystal, her mother's early birthday gift. She dangled it from its string so it would throw flashing bars of rainbow colors in all directions. It made Maggie smile to remember what her mother had called it: "Pocket magic."

The voice of the captain filled the cabin: "Flight

attendants please prepare for landing."

The plane slid further toward the coast, then over the ocean itself. That morning Maggie had looked down on the Pacific. Here was the Atlantic. Coast to coast in one day. The realization gave her goose bumps.

Stuffing the crystal back into her pocket, Maggie gazed at the sea and, as always, tried to think in magical ways. Things *were* better that way. So she decided the water was like a roughened silver plate, while the speedboat trailing a feathery white wake was the fingertip of Neptune, the Roman sea god, making his long, drawnout signature.

Right across from where Maggie sat, up by the door, the flight attendant named Karen—she had told Maggie to call her that—buckled herself tightly into a special seat and flashed a smile.

"Be there soon, hon," Karen said.

Maggie, wishing the woman would not always say "honey," or "hon," nonetheless returned the smile before looking out the window again. Now they were swinging sharply and the sound of the airplane changed, becoming loud. There was a sudden bump. Maggie closed her eyes: "I'm on a magic carpet," she told herself. "The bumps are the snatching hands of goblins trying to shake me loose." Only when she felt a tap on her knee did she open her eyes.

"The wheels lowering," Karen informed her. "Now remember, honey, we'll wait until everyone is out before

I take you to Dad. It'll be your dad who'll be meeting you, right?"

Maggie nodded.

"When did you see him last?"

"Christmas."

"Oh, you must miss him so."

"I do."

For a moment Maggie wanted to tell Karen how nervous she was.

"What's he do?"

"Business," Maggie said vaguely. It was something about insurance. She was not sure.

"Oh, you're going to have such a *good* time," Karen said.

Karen's words were the same her mother had used. Why, Maggie wondered, did people say things like that? Did it mean that if she had a rotten time it would be her fault? All the same she felt obliged to reply, "I know."

Then quickly she added, "My father rented a log cabin cottage on a pond, well, lake actually, for August. I've never been there, but he said it's on the water and cool."

"Lucky you. Can you swim?"

"Yes. I'll be thirteen in three weeks."

"A teenager!"

Maggie blushed and turned away, asking herself why she'd wanted to tell her age. Instead of answering her question, she peered down into people's backyards.

Someone was getting a suntan. Kids were splashing in a turquoise-colored pool.

Suddenly, before she could prepare herself, the runway was close and getting closer. It must have been this way, Maggie told herself, when Dorothy landed in Oz. But the next moment the plane landed with hardly a bump.

Karen spoke into the phone by her seat, filling the cabin with her voice. "Welcome to Providence, Rhode Island. The local time is five-o-five, Eastern standard time. The temperature is ninety-six."

Some of the people in the cabin groaned.

Karen winked at Maggie. "Please remain in your seats with your seat belts fastened until the captain has brought the plane to a complete stop.

"On behalf of Captain Wooten and your entire Chicago-based flight crew, we want to thank you for flying United Airlines and hope to see you all real soon."

Karen hung up the phone and leaned out of her seat toward Maggie.

"Just a few minutes, hon."

Suddenly Maggie missed her mom. Her home. Her friends. Maybe Joanna would not want her around now that she had a baby of her own. Maybe the baby would cry all the time and be a pill. Maybe the baby would not like her. Maybe her dad had asked her to come only because that was the agreement he and her mom had made when they divorced long ago, but now he really did not want her. Maybe she would be sick. For the second time Maggie wished nothing had changed.

"Okay, honey, time to get all your stuff together. Your dad will be waiting and wondering."

Maggie shoveled books, map, portable cassette player, and tapes into her backpack, grabbed her jacket, then hurried out along the exit ramp. Half skipping, half walking, she tried to act cool, though she knew she was excited. As the waiting lobby came into view, Karen touched her shoulder.

"Go, honey!" she whispered. Maggie was running now, pushing through the glass doors, looking everywhere in the crowd for her father. He was not there.

CHAPTER

2

"We'll just wait here a moment, hon," Karen said. "Don't you worry. Your dad must have gotten tied up in traffic somewhere."

Maggie felt as if she had missed a step at the bottom of the stairs. She was falling but there was no point in crying until she landed. *If* she landed. She kept looking around, thinking her father had to be there somewhere.

"Maggie!"

Maggie swung around. Joanna, baby in arms, was working hard to get through the crowd.

"My stepmother," Maggie explained to Karen, trying to push away the disappointment she felt.

"Hi!" Joanna called again, breathless as she reached them. She was a pretty woman, dark, and taller than

Maggie's father as well as considerably younger. Maggie always wanted to know how much younger—Joanna had been her father's secretary—but never had the nerve to ask.

"How awful for you," Joanna said, all breathless. "Have you been waiting long?"

"Just got here," Maggie replied, trying to get a look at the baby.

"Are you Mrs. Lavchek?" Karen asked. Maggie heard disapproval in the voice, but she herself was too busy sorting out her reaction to Linda, who was smaller than she thought she'd be, with thin wisps of curly blond hair, a little pink mouth, and dark eyes.

"Sure am. Oh, Maggie, I'm real sorry we're late."

"Caught in traffic?" Karen asked.

Joanna nodded. "Her dad wrote instructions, but I got mixed up." She appealed to Maggie. "You know what his handwriting is like."

Maggie, looking up at Joanna, made an effort to smile.

Karen offered a clipboard and Joanna signed the necessary papers. Then the flight attendant went off, but not before bending over Maggie and whispering, "Be good now. And happy birthday!"

Maggie, watching her walk away, was unexpectedly sorry to see her go.

"Maggie?"

Maggie turned.

"Here's little Linda," Joanna said, grinning.

Maggie looked at the baby again, attempting to read some character, some personality on the bland face.

Joanna wiggled the baby's arm in a greeting. "Hello, Maggie," she mimicked.

Suddenly the baby's face blossomed into a broad grin. To Maggie's surprise, a pang of jealously shot through her. Embarrassed, she stared at the baby, then tentatively reached out a finger. Linda grasped it—then belched.

Maggie and Joanna laughed. The laughter broke the tension.

"Where's Dad?" Maggie wanted to know.

"He was just walking out the door when the phone rang," Joanna explained. "Someone at the office—I guess. Well, you know your father. That's where he's really at. Anyway, he asked me to come. He's very upset he couldn't."

"Oh."

"Don't be mad at him."

"Okay," Maggie replied. But Joanna's remark made her aware that she was mad.

"Come on, let's see you!" Joanna cried. "You're taller. Prettier. And almost thirteen."

Maggie, not unpleased, blushed.

"What do you think of this little bundle?" Joanna hefted Linda in her arms.

"Cute," Maggie said, aware how inadequate that was.

"See what she's wearing?"

Only then did Maggie realize the baby was wearing the summer suit she'd sent when Linda was born. Understanding that she was meant to be pleased, she smiled up at Joanna.

"You have more stuff, don't you?" Joanna asked.

"Couple of things."

"Let's go get 'em."

The bags came through quickly. With Maggie lugging her suitcase with two hands and Joanna manipulating the baby as well as a small duffel bag, they went through the revolving doors to the outside. The moment they did they were smothered by a blanket of humid heat.

"Yuk!" Maggie groaned.

"Welcome to the Northeast. Honest, it's a lot better down by the lake. You must be tired. Come on. The car is right over there. It's got air-conditioning."

Maggie halted. "My mom said to call when I got here."

"How about doing it from the cabin? Then you'll really be there. Besides, your dad will be fretting to see you. He's planned this fantastic New England banquet. Lobster, corn, tomatoes, local ice cream."

"I never ate lobster."

"He said you'll love it."

"Okay," Maggie said, though she was not so sure.

In moments they were heading east on the highway with the baby asleep in her car chair.

"How far is it?" Maggie asked.

"Not long. How's your ma?"

Maggie pushed herself back in her seat. She always felt uncomfortable when either of her parents asked about the other parent, convinced they only did it to make *her* feel better. It had the opposite effect. And when Joanna asked, she almost resented it. "Fine" was all she replied.

Joanna said no more. But as though to rebuke Joanna, Maggie noticed that her stepmother was not so carefully dressed as she had always been before. Her hair had an uncombed look. Her makeup was slapdash. Even her clothing was rumpled.

They went through Providence, then passed a sign that said MASSACHUSETTS WELCOMES YOU.

Joanna said, "Maggie, I hope you'll get to love your sister."

The word *sister*, said so matter-of-factly, brought Maggie's mind back to where she was. "Sister?" she echoed.

"I know, half sister. But I hate that word, don't you? Like stepsister. Another dumb word. So let's just say sister. She smiles all the time. And sleeps a lot, including right through the night."

Maggie, not knowing what to say, watched the passing scenery. She saw green marsh grass, water, boats. "Is that the ocean?" she asked.

"We're running right along the coast, so it must be connected some way."

Conversation flagged. They drove in silence. Then Joanna said, "How'd you do in school this term?"

That seemed like old news to Maggie, and besides, she was certain she'd told her father. Apparently, he had said nothing to Joanna. "I got an A in everything except French." Maggie made a face. "I only got a C for that."

"I didn't know you were taking French."

"I told Dad."

"I took French in college. Would you believe, six years ago I was in college. Now look at me. Anyway, I never learned it. Not really. Except stuff like *Parlez-vous français?*"

Maggie shook her head and looked out the window.

"Maggie, I'm real glad you're here," Joanna said, surprising Maggie with the emotion in her voice. "It's going to be *so* good having you around." She reached out, took Maggie's hand, and squeezed it.

Maggie squeezed back but did not know how to reply.

Then, after a moment, Joanna said, "And your dad's sure to feel better with his new medication."

Maggie's stomach gave a little flip. "I didn't know something was the matter."

Joanna was silent for a moment. Then she said, "Didn't he talk to you about his health?"

"No."

"He promised he would."

"Is something the matter?" Maggie asked.

"Nothing serious. He's had some heart palpitations."

"Is that bad?"

"No. Not really. He has this medication which he's taking. As long as he does, and avoids certain kinds of food, blah, blah, we're fine. Of course we have to be on the lookout for certain signs. Trouble is, Alan likes to pretend he's younger than fifty. Your dad isn't exactly great about taking things easy. Always hard on himself. You know that."

Maggie did not know. No more than she knew what to say. She sensed that Joanna was talking to her as an adult. She liked that, felt flattered, but all the same, she wished it had been her father who'd told her.

"I think kids need to know such things," Joanna chatted on. "I was an army brat, you know. You wake up and boom, no warning, you've just switched countries. I hated that. Anyway, I don't want you to worry. I'm not."

Maggie glanced over to Joanna and wondered if that "I'm not" was accurate. It did not quite sound true. Ruefully, Maggie stared out the window and recalled her airplane wish that things might stay as they always had. She put her hand into her pocket, closed her eyes, squeezed the glass crystal, then said to herself, "I'm in a pink coral coach pulled by sixteen silver horses, racing over the slipping sands of time."

But when she opened her eyes she was in an air-conditioned car and Joanna—her stepmother—was driving while her half sister lay asleep in the backseat. And her father? Maggie did not want to think about him. But she knew that—contrary to Joanna's suggestion—she was worried.

CHAPTER

3

They sped over the Fall River Bridge, passed through the city of the same name, turned onto another highway for a few miles, then suddenly were moving along an ordinary road. Farm fields and small houses were on all sides.

"Just three miles from here," Joanna said.

Maggie sat straighter.

A left turn brought them down a hill and over a small causeway.

"Sawdy Pond," Joanna announced.

Before Maggie could take it in, the car slowed and turned onto a rutted dirt road that ran through woods. Here and there Maggie could see collapsed rock walls that wove among trees while white bars of sunlight probed the cool green air. An occasional flower bloomed unexpectedly—candlelike in the woody gloom—while overhead, tree branches interlocked in patterns that reminded Maggie of her mother's intricate knitting. She loved what she was seeing.

"Quarter of a mile," Joanna said. She spoke in a whisper.

A rabbit leaped out in front of the car.

"Oooh!" Maggie cried. "Don't hit it!"

Joanna braked. Though the car was going no more than a few miles an hour, the rabbit became frantic, darting from one side of the road to the other in a confused attempt to escape.

"To the side, dummy!" Maggie shouted at the rabbit. "The side!"

The rabbit, as if finally hearing, dove into roadside undergrowth.

Relieved, Maggie slumped back. "It was so panicky." To her surprise she found herself suppressing a desire to cry.

Joanna continued on, and the road narrowed even more. After a sharp right turn around some boulders she brought the car to a stop.

Maggie looked about. On three sides were trees. But off to the left was a small log cabin. Beyond was a patch of lawn, then water.

"Welcome to Finn's Lodge."

"Finn?"

"Owner's name." Joanna tooted the horn twice.

Alan Lavchek, Maggie's father, thickset, balding, but with a round, youthful face, came out the screen door and stood on the side deck, smiling broadly. A portable phone was pressed to his ear. Though dressed in jeans, running shoes, and a T-shirt that read "Aged to Perfection," he looked impeccably neat.

Maggie climbed out of the car.

"Look, Mr. Simmons," her father was saying into the phone. "I have to go. My beautiful daughter just arrived. I haven't seen her in half a year. Exactly. Look, I appreciate your help. Really. Things will work out fine. Nothing to worry about. Really, I have to go. Goodbye!" He took the phone from his ear and held out his arms.

Maggie ran and hugged him, allowing herself to be hugged.

"Hey! Hey! Hey!" her father cried, lifting her off her feet. "Am I happy to see you!" He hugged her again. "Sorry I couldn't be there." He looked to Joanna. "Any problems?"

"A few minutes late."

He wagged a finger at her. "Told you you should have left early. Well, anyway, you got a chance to meet Linda," he said, turning back to Maggie. "Ain't she a beaut? But not as beautiful as you are!"

Maggie hugged him again, not knowing which feeling was strongest in her, anger that he had not come to meet her, the love she felt for him, or concern. Unable to deal with the tumble of emotions, she broke away and ran across the lawn until she stood at the lake's edge.

Though the lake was big—more than a mile to the far side and half again as wide—she could still make out a few houses hidden shyly among trees by the shores. Here and there lumpish boulders broke the water surface, water that sparkled beneath the slanted gleaming of a lowering sun. Close to shore, blades of grass spiked up through the water. A barn swallow dove for gnats. Nearby was a little wooden dock and tied to it, a canoe, its paddles neatly tucked within.

Maggie turned to the right. There seemed to be an inlet there—how big it was or where it led she could not tell—with waves of marsh grass moving gently under the soft stroke of a teasing breeze. It was all very calm. All very beautiful. And, she decided with a catch of breath, very magical.

To Maggie's surprise her heart began to pound. Once again her eyes filled with tears. But why she felt that way, she did not know.

A hand touched her shoulder. She turned. It was her father.

"Pretty as a picture," he said loudly. "Isn't it?"

Maggie, wishing he would see it as something more than that, smiled up at him, then turned back to the lake. Even as she did, an enormous gray-blue bird rose out from the marsh. Neck and head curled back against itself, long yellow beak thrust forward, legs trailing, the bird beat the air with its great wings.

Maggie gasped. "What's that?" she cried.

"Great blue heron. It lives to the back of the cabin, in the marsh. Hey," he said, giving her shoulder an affectionate shake, "sorry Joanna was late. She takes forever to get ready. And, now, with the baby. . . . And you know how people call me all the time. Even here. Believe me, I hate it. Anyway, I know my Maggie. Always reasonable."

Maggie, wondering if she was reasonable, shrugged. How often had her mother told her she did not reason enough?

"You need to call your mom," Mr. Lavchek reminded her. "And Joanna will have dinner ready. Come on." He turned, then paused. "Kid, I wish you knew how glad I am to see you," he said.

Maggie took her father's proffered hand and allowed herself to be led toward he cabin. She wished she knew how glad he was to see her, too.

CHAPTER

4

When Maggie called Seattle, her mother answered on the first ring.

"Hi, Mom," Maggie said into the phone. "I'm here."

"Any problems?"

"No."

"Your father meet you okay?"

"Yes."

"I'm missing you already."

"I'm missing you."

"Is it pretty there?"

"Yes."

"Hot?"

"Not here."

"What's the place like?"

Maggie looked about the cabin. It really was very

small, just one big room, its walls and ceiling covered with wood. At one end were a stone fireplace, a coffee table piled with her father's papers, plus a folding couch and some easy chairs. One wall had a tattered calendar from a year long gone. On another wall was a cheap print. A cradle and changing table for the baby had been set up in a corner. The air smelt of talcum powder and slightly sour milk.

Small as the room was, it was divided by a wooden island that served as kitchen table, for at the other end of the same room was the kitchen. A toilet room was just off the kitchen. The shower stall was outside, at the end of the side deck.

Facing the lawn and lake was a screened-in porch. It had a long table and chairs, plus a shelf with old books, a few box games, a pack of cards.

Maggie wondered where she was going to sleep.

"Maggie? You there?" her mother said, breaking into her thoughts. "What's it like?"

"I can't describe it," Maggie said. "Not now. I'll write you."

"How's your dad?"

"Okay," Maggie said.

"And Joanna?"

"Fine."

"What's the baby like?"

"Nice." Maggie glanced up. It was impossible to talk to her mother with her father—and Joanna—looking on, even though they were making an effort to appear as if they were not listening.

"I'll let you go," Maggie's mother said. "You must be tired. Now, remember, call me anytime you want. *Anytime*. If I'm not here the message box will be on. Remember, if it says, 'I can't get to the phone right now,' that means I've gone someplace. But if it says, 'It's not *possible* to answer the phone right now,' I'll be at school, and you can reach me there. Okay?" Maggie's mother was the resident nurse-practitioner at a community college.

"Okay."

"Bye. Regards to all. I love you."

"I love you, too."

Maggie hung up. Her dad turned around. "Everything okay?"

"Yes."

"Hungry for dinner?"

"I think so."

"Great. Water's a-boiling." He looked to Joanna, who was sitting in one of the easy chairs, nursing the baby. "Be ready soon?" he asked her.

"She's just about done."

Maggie, who had never observed a baby being nursed before, watched, fascinated. She found herself wondering if she would ever do that and at the thought, blushed.

"Hey, Maggie," her father cried.

Maggie turned, and cringed.

Her father was dangling a reddish brown creature with many legs and claws waving frantically. The first thing Maggie thought of was a spider. "What *is* that?" she cried.

"Lobster."

"What are you *doing* with it?"

"I'm about to drop it in the boiling water."

"Alive?"

"It doesn't hurt it."

"How do you know?"

"Don't be sentimental. It's a false emotion. Bad for the brain. Bad for the soul. Now, want to do it?"

"No!" Maggie turned her back on her father and watched Joanna and the baby. Joanna was gazing lovingly into Linda's face.

"Here goes!" her father shouted. "Three of them!"

Maggie closed her eyes and did not open them until she had counted three splashes.

"Dinner in fifteen minutes," her father announced.

Dinner—out on the porch table, surrounded by insect repellent candles—was a small riot. After insisting they all wear bibs, Mr. Lavchek demonstrated the proper way to eat lobsters. You had to tear the now brilliant red creatures apart, cutting through shell and many spidery legs, using hands, fingers, teeth, scissors, and nutcrackers, as well as tiny forks to poke, pry, bite, cut, and suck all the meat out, dip it into butter, then stuff it into your mouth.

At first disgusted, Maggie gradually began to see the fun of it all. Even when her fingers were dirty and butter dribbled down her chin, she had to admit the taste was something great.

Then there was corn on the cob—Silver Queen, her father called it, "the best"—dripping butter, salt, and pepper, while the great slabs of scarlet ripe tomatoes, sprinkled with fresh basil, contributed to the lovely mess.

"August in New England," Mr. Lavchek exulted. "Best food in the world!"

With the baby asleep in the cradle, Joanna was equally into the meal, laughing and telling stories. In fact it got so raucous Joanna had to remind them the baby was asleep. And then Maggie and her father started to exchange knock-knock jokes.

"Knock knock," Mr. Lavchek said.

"Who's there?"

"Amos."

"Amos who?"

"Amos-quito bit me."

"That's so *dumb*!" Maggie cried, loving it, and shouting, "Knock knock!"

"Who's there?"

"Sam and Janet!"

"Sam and Janet who?"

Maggie bounced to her feet and, placing her hand to her bib, sang out, "Sam and Janet evening . . ."

Joanna, who had gotten up to shut the door to the main room, groaned.

"Do you know why people groan at puns?" Mr. Lavchek said.

Maggie shook her head.

"Speech, professor," Joanna said. "Speech!"

Mr. Lavchek frowned. But then he said, "Punning is a form of humor that requires a linguistic skill that few people have. Ergo, they belittle puns so as to hide their ignorance. In short, jealousy."

"Oh-oh," Joanna said with a wink at Maggie, "I think I've just been knocked down by a hit-and-run lecture."

"It so happens I'm correct!" Mr. Lavchek snapped.

Maggie winced at his anger. That was the end of the jokes. And halfway through the bowl of locally made ginger ice cream, Maggie felt as if an enormous weight had settled over her eyes. She felt herself nodding.

"Somebody has had a long day," Joanna said kindly.

"Hey," Mr. Lavchek protested, "what about the movie I picked out at the mall? First day together, movie. Isn't that the rule? *The Sword of King Arthur.* Thought you'd be up for it."

Maggie appealed to Joanna with a look.

"Alan, she's too tired. And to tell the truth, so am I."

"That so?" Mr. Lavchek asked Maggie.

Maggie nodded.

"How about a game of Monopoly then?" He gestured to Joanna. "She refuses to play."

"Alan, I don't enjoy money games."

"Because you always lose," Mr. Lavchek explained to Maggie. "She's got insufficient ambition."

"I married you," Joanna said quickly. "What does that make you?"

"Good question," Mr. Lavchek shot back. "What's your pleasure?" he said to Maggie.

"Maybe tomorrow," she replied.

"Okay. But remember, it's the two of you who are the wimps, not me."

Maggie frowned.

"What's the matter?" he demanded.

"Nothing," she said. But even as she said it, she knew she needed to be alone. "Where am I sleeping?" she asked.

"I'll show you."

Mr. Lavchek led her into the cottage and pointed up at the ceiling over the kitchen area. Only then did Maggie realize it was much lower than the rest of the house. And there was a door there.

Her father opened a narrow closet and slid out a ladder. He climbed up and pulled open the door, then came down.

"Go take a look."

Maggie went up the ladder and gazed into a tiny loft. There was no room to stand up—just enough to sit— but a mattress had been laid out and made. A little radio had been placed by the side of the bed along with a reading lamp and flashlight. The lamp illuminated a row of stuffed fantasy creatures propped up against the pillow. Merlin the Magician. Glinda, the good witch. A unicorn and a dragon. A hobbit. These were Maggie's; some she had bought with her father, others had been gifts from him. They all stayed in his Boston house. With their big round eyes they looked as if they had been waiting for her. Maggie was moved to see them so.

"Do you like it?" her father called up.

"Love it," she shouted.

Ready for sleep in her pink nightshirt, Maggie climbed down to hug and kiss her father good-night. When Joanna held out her arms, Maggie hesitated briefly, but when Joanna coaxed her with a smile and said, "Come on," Maggie hugged her, too, then turned and fled up the ladder.

First she hung her crystal from a splinter on an overhead beam. Then, after carefully arranging the magical folk around her—like an adoring audience—she crawled under the sheet. Her father—only his head visible above the ladder—smiled and said, "Night-night. Don't let the bedbugs bite," just as he had when she was little.

"Dad!" she objected, "I'm almost thirteen!" But she was happy he had said it.

"I love you," he called.

"I love you, too," she echoed as he shut the loft door.

Maggie, alone for the first time that day, lay quietly, content simply to be where she was, gazing at the crystal and its flashing rainbow colors. She listened to the sounds from below, the soft murmurs of her father and Joanna. They were doing dishes. But as she listened she realized they were arguing.

Maggie felt instant uneasiness. What were they arguing about? Was she the cause? She tried to make sense of their words. It sounded as if Joanna was angry at her father.

Maggie sighed. She liked Joanna. In some ways she was easier to be with than her father. Was that disloyal to her father? To her own mother?

Not wanting to think about such things, Maggie turned off the light. "Oh!" she cried. Right over her head was a skylight. She could see the stars.

Now she heard music. It was her father's, she knew, because he liked what he called "doo-wop music," music from the fifties, groups who sang without back-up instruments.

As the voices rose and fell, as they swelled and carried her along, Maggie had the sensation of being cast adrift upon the universe, of flying utterly free. Maggie remembered the heron she had seen by the lake. It appeared in her mind like a solitary, slowly flowing phantom, one of the most beautiful, mysterious things she had ever seen.

Why, she asked herself, did thinking of the heron

make her sad? She reached for the stuffed figure of Merlin the Magician, the oldest of her magic people— and hugged him. To her surprise his smell was familiar, reminding her of when she had been young. Exactly how young had she been when she got him? Five? Six? Why couldn't she remember? Thinking more about the question than the answer, Maggie fell asleep.

CHAPTER 5

Maggie woke up uncertain where she was. There were no street sounds. No sounds of her mother moving about. Not even the smell of strong coffee. But then a rooster crowed. Once, twice, three times, and Maggie remembered: She was in Westport. By the lake. With her father. And it was dawn.

She rolled over and looked up. The patch of sky she saw was neither dark nor light, but gray. She sat up and listened. The rooster crowed again. A bird trilled.

Needing to go to the toilet, Maggie crawled to the edge of the loft and tapped the door open with a toe. She looked down. The cabin was suffused with light. The baby slept in her cradle. The couch had been opened and her father and Joanna, under covers, were fast asleep, too, arms around each other. A sense of shock went through Maggie to see them so. Then she found herself giggling and decided they were sort of sweet.

Backing out of the loft, Maggie found the ladder rungs with her feet. She climbed down quietly and tiptoed to the toilet. When she came out, she turned to the ladder but stopped when she heard the trill of the bird again.

She stepped out on the side deck. A mist—cool, damp, and gray—hung over the lake and eddied over the lawn, even swirling gently about her. It reminded Maggie of the spun glass people put around Christmas trees. The mist softened everything she saw, blending trees to sky, sky to cabin. It was as if she were standing at the core of a pearl, looking out at the world through milky silver.

The rooster crowed again. The bird called, too. This time Maggie saw it hopping on the lawn but was disappointed to see that it was small and rather dull to look at.

But it did remind her of the blue heron. Recalling that her father said the bird lived in the marsh, she looked about, wondering if it was awake. Between where she stood and where he'd said the marsh was were trees. A path led through them.

Maggie stepped off the deck and onto the wet, cold grass. She shivered but felt only pleasure in the sensation.

She moved among the trees. It was dark, but the darkness was not frightening, only somber and soft. Puffs of mist—like the ghosts of mushrooms—blossomed from the ground. A blood-red salamander rested on dark green moss and held still for a moment before slithering off. But Maggie had seen its tiny toes. Counted them. That, too, was a thrill.

She walked on. Another bird called. A rabbit squatted on the path before her, nose wiggling, jaws working hard, dark almond eyes staring at Maggie. Maggie stared back, wondering if it was the same rabbit she'd seen on the road the day before. Did it know how close to death it had been?

Soon the trees began to thin and then, very quickly, Maggie found herself on the edge of the marsh. It was brighter there. Yet the mist was thicker, too, erratic, a kaleidoscope of gray, silver, and white, shifting in and out of focus. Maggie could not see the far side of the marsh. What she did see were patches of marsh grass rising straight and green amid dark, shallow waters. A red-winged blackbird, flashing rosy epaulets, darted by, calling, "kouk-la-ree, kouk-la-ree." The angular form of a tree appeared, only to become lost again in the mist. A bubble burst with a gulp. Was it a bullfrog? Then she saw—not twenty-five feet from where she stood—the blue heron.

The great bird—it was more than four feet tall—seemed to have stepped directly out of the mist. Or perhaps the mist had pulled away to reveal it. Like magic. Now it was standing upon two stalk legs, sinuous neck curled so that its long, daggerlike beak and round, lemon-colored eyes could stare down into shallow waters.

Its back and wings were gray-blue. Its head was white. But the head had a masklike stripe of black feathers, which extended into a tufted plume, a flowing crown.

With awe, Maggie watched. Never before had she been so close to such a big and wild bird. How beautiful it was. How still. It was the stillness that seemed most wonderful. The only thing moving was the crown of head feathers, gently stirred by teasing currents of air.

With exquisite slowness, the heron lifted one leg out of the water, shifted it forward, then set it down. Then, just as slowly, it moved the other leg. It was as if time itself had slowed. Having moved, the bird stood absolutely still again. Maggie wondered what it was waiting for so patiently. She dared not move herself.

Realizing she had been holding her breath, Maggie swallowed. When she did the heron suddenly stretched its neck straight up and, beak pointing skyward, kept it there as if listening. "Frahnk!" it suddenly cried, deep and harsh. "Frahnk!"

Maggie was sure the bird had caught some sense of her. Had become alarmed. She tried to suppress her own breathing sounds.

As though coming back to life, the heron slowly lowered its neck and began to peer into the water again.

The next instant the bird plunged its beak into the water and then withdrew it. Maggie thought she saw a tiny fish tail wiggle in the bird's beak. It happened so quickly— all in a blur—she could not be sure.

The heron—motionless again—was staring down as before.

Maggie was afraid to move. But she could not stay so still, not like the bird. She shifted her feet. The heron's head shot up. Once again, it was listening, watching. Involuntarily, Maggie cleared her throat.

At the sound the bird spread its enormous wings and, with a rush of wind that Maggie felt on her eyes, the bird leaped into the air and flew away, its wings flapping slowly, voluptuously.

The day brightened, revealing the sky as a layer cake of multicolored clouds. Momentarily, the treetops seemed to blaze while the woods behind sang with the cacophony of birds. On her bare arms Maggie felt the kiss of moist, warm air. A sense of pleasure filled her.

Reluctantly, Maggie walked back to the cottage, entered with caution, and climbed into the loft. As she lay in her bed she kept thinking of the heron. How beautiful it was. How magical. Never before had she experienced such a sense of magic, real magic.

Maggie picked up her figure of Merlin the Magician and stared at him. His button eyes stared back blankly. Maggie put him aside and curled under her sheet. Then she drifted off to sleep. . . .

CHAPTER
6

Maggie did not tell her father and Joanna about her dawn adventure. At first she simply forgot, and then it seemed like a dream. But even when she did remember she decided she would rather not tell. She was not sure why she made that decision. Embarrassment, partly. What was she to say, that she needed to go to the toilet? And how could she explain *why* she went for a walk? No reason, really. As for what she had seen or felt when she looked at the heron, well, they might tease her. Besides, in the bright, hot sun, it did seem a little foolish.

In any case, that first morning was full. A big breakfast, cleanup, planning for the day. And at almost every step along the way, the baby needed attending.

"Lots of work, isn't it?" Joanna said to Maggie as she changed Linda's diapers for the third time that morning.

Maggie wrinkled her nose.

"You get used to it awful fast," Joanna said, as if reading her mind. "This part just stops mattering. Want to learn how to change her?"

"How about later?" Mr. Lavchek called from across the room. "I thought I'd take Maggie out in the canoe."

Joanna said, "Alan, we need to do some food shopping."

"It can wait," Mr. Lavchek said.

"As long as it gets done," Joanna said.

"Give me a break," Maggie's father snapped. "I get to spend a few weeks a year with her."

Maggie froze. Joanna, her face red, bent over the baby and said nothing.

"Hey, kid," Mr. Lavchek said to Maggie, "don't just stand there. Get your bathing suit on!"

Maggie, trying not to think about the exchange between her father and Joanna, was in the loft putting on her suit when she realized she had not been asked if *she* wanted to go. She paused. She remembered now; her father had a knack for knowing what she wanted to do. That she liked. Except he would tell her before she could say it for herself. That she found annoying. Which was exactly what had happened. She did want to go on the lake but wished he had asked her. She decided she would try to say something. But when she climbed down, her father was on the front porch, talking on the telephone. A pile of papers lay before him.

"Now, sir," he was saying into the phone, "when I spoke to you last week . . . Wait a minute, hold on." He put the phone aside and turned to Maggie. "Why don't you wait outside? I'll be there in two minutes." He picked up the phone again. "Mr. Harrison. Okay. Let me explain what I'm offering to do for you . . ."

Frustrated, Maggie wandered out along the lawn to the lake's edge and stepped onto the little wooden dock that jutted over the water. She looked down. Small fish were flitting about in the warm shallows. Kneeling, she watched them. Some of the fish were as big as four inches. Most were smaller. They were all gray-green, save their fins, which were blue and constantly fluttering. Sometimes the fish hovered. Other moments they darted away. Maggie watched, fascinated.

It was half an hour later when Mr. Lavchek appeared. "There you are!" he called. "Been looking all over for you."

"Dad, I've been right here."

"Now look, kid, I can't control these calls. They're important. We going out in the canoe or not?"

"If you want to."

"Of course I want to. Come on. Don't pout. It makes you ugly. Let's go."

Maggie, trying not to show her hurt, allowed herself to be helped into the bow of the canoe while Mr. Lavchek went into the stern.

"Do you know how to paddle?"

"No."

"Well, we're running late. Joanna will throw a fit if I don't do the shopping soon. I'll paddle for now. Teach you later. Okay?"

"Okay."

"Ready, set. Here we go."

The canoe slid out onto the lake. Maggie kept her eyes on the water ahead.

"You're angry," Maggie heard her father say.

"Yes," she felt compelled to answer.

"Then just say it. Sulking rots the soul."

"I did say it."

"Maggie, I am sorry. This isn't a good time for me."

Maggie became alarmed. "Why? What do you mean?"

Her father became thoughtful. All he said, however, was, "Too complicated."

"Why is it complicated?"

"Because I say so."

Maggie did not know how to reply. But the silence that had fallen between them made her uncomfortable. After a while, she said, "Is this fresh water?"

"Absolutely," her father answered, brisk and knowing again. "Even though we're only a few miles from the ocean. That's why we get that constant breeze. As for this, it's a glacier lake. Formed thousands of years ago by a retreating glacier. All those boulders you see in the lake. Same thing. Glacial deposits. Terminal moraine."

"What's that mean, moraine?"

"Moraine. Boulders, gravel, dirt, carried by a glacier. And terminal means 'the end.' "

"Like—terminal illness," Maggie said, the words just popping out.

For a moment her father said nothing. Then he murmured, "I suppose." Once again a silence came between them, thick enough, Maggie felt, that she might paddle through it. She said, "Can you go fishing here?"

"Oh, sure."

"Do you like to?"

"What?"

"Fish."

"Boring."

Mr. Lavchek paddled on. Now it was he who spoke. "Hey, kid!" he called. "I'm awful glad you're here."

"So am I," Maggie said lamely as she scanned a far shore, eyeing houses. "Do you know any of the people who live in those places?"

"Not a soul, I'm glad to say. You're stuck with me."

She let her father paddle. Keeping her eyes forward, she said, "Joanna said your heart isn't so good."

Her father did not reply.

She looked back over her shoulder. "Is that true?" she persisted.

Mr. Lavchek was scowling. "I asked her not to say anything. Joanna tends to worry. But it's nothing. Come on, kid. Loosen up. This is vacation time. And it cost a fortune. So you don't have permission to worry. Hey, you still like magic, don't you? Let me show you something special." He abruptly turned the canoe about.

"Where we going?"

"To the marsh."

"It's a bit of a trick to get in," her father said. "There's a channel. There, see it? Leads to a big marsh."

Maggie spied what looked like a passage between the boulders. Beyond was an open area.

"Maybe we'll see that heron," her father said. "Proper name, great blue heron. In Latin, *Ardea herodias.* Often miscalled a crane. Range is southern Canada to Mexico. Winters in South America. Habitat: marshes, swamps, shores, tidal flats."

Maggie glanced back admiringly. "How can you remember things like that?"

He grinned. "As a client once told me, I've got a photogenic memory."

"That heron we saw, is that the only one here?" Maggie asked.

"They all look pretty much the same to me."

The canoe moved forward. The water passage became narrow, snakelike. Very soon though they were out of the channel and in what almost seemed to be another lake. It was the marsh. Maggie found it unexpectedly large though they were surrounded by water lilies, perfectly round green leaves that had her thinking of a floating polka-dot carpet. Here and there white and yellow flowers grew among the leaves, their petals bringing to mind clusters of fingers. Small islands—bush or grass covered—dotted the water surface. A few dead trees—trunks blackened, branches without leaves—seemed to have grown right out of the water.

Maggie caught a glimpse of a house through the foliage that crowded the edges of the far side of the marsh. But the canoe shifted before she could be sure. She was about to ask her father about it when she spied the heron. It was sitting, unmoving, on the limb of a dead tree at the very edge of the marsh. It looked like a ghost.

". . . but you'll see," she heard her father say, as though from distant space, "the baby will look to you for answers to everything. It's a big responsibility."

Maggie could pay attention to nothing but the heron. She knew she should tell her father what she was seeing. Share it. But she was still angry at him and did not want to.

"Maggie?"

"What?"

"Did you hear me?"

Maggie forced herself to turn about. "I'm sorry."

"What were you staring at so raptly?"

"I thought I saw something."

"Well, I was just saying how important you're going to be for Linda. A terrific role model."

"Oh . . ." Maggie said. She turned back to look at the heron. The tree was there but not the bird. It had vanished. Suddenly she was not certain she had seen it.

"Maggie!" her father called impatiently. "I'm *trying* to have a serious talk with you!"

"Did you see anything there?" Maggie asked, pointing.

"Where? What?"

"On that tree."

"What?"

Maggie could read the irritation in her father's voice over being interrupted. "Nothing," she said.

"I'm a little nearsighted. I should have put in my contacts."

"I didn't know you wore them."

Her father made a gesture of annoyance. "Happens," he said.

Maggie turned back to gaze at the tree, wishing the bird would return.

"Anyway," her father was saying, "I'd like you to

spend some quality time with Linda. One of the problems of our modern age is that young people—like you—don't experience true family life and its responsibilities, which is what babies are all about.

"You're going to be different. And you need not worry. Joanna will teach you everything you should know. Actually, she's quite competent. You'll see how quickly the baby bonds with you. When you have kids of your own, you'll be grateful."

"Maybe I won't have any."

"You will."

Maggie knew she should reply. Say something. Assert her independence. But her mind went back to seeing the heron. Or, she reminded herself, what she had thought she'd seen.

"Do you believe in omens?" she abruptly asked.

"Omens?" Mr. Lavchek was taken aback.

Maggie felt herself blushing. She had not meant to ask such a thing. But all the same, she felt she needed to know. "Yes, omens."

"Prophecy? Something that portends good or evil?"

"I guess."

"Omens—so-called—are merely events or things which persons—unconsciously—desire to happen."

"Oh."

"Like that dead tree, death. Or those water lilies, life. But, do you remember that heron we saw yesterday?"

Maggie was startled that her father was telling her

exactly what she wanted to know. "Yes . . ."

"The heron is thought to be an omen for two things."

"What?"

"Life. But also, death. You take your pick—according to your desire. So, no, I don't believe in them. What makes you ask?"

"I don't know," Maggie said, conscious that she was not telling the truth.

The rest of the morning was spent doing very little. There was talk about an expedition to the beach, but Joanna reminded everyone there was shopping to do first.

At that Maggie's father announced, "I've got some calls to make." So saying, he took himself out to a lawn chair. With papers and portable phone in hand he began to work.

Joanna watched him. Maggie could see how nettled she was. After a moment she turned to Maggie.

"Up for a little baby-sitting?" she asked. "Don't worry. Linda will sleep right through. And if she wakes you can give her this bottle."

Maggie, not knowing what else to do, agreed. As it worked out, Joanna was right. Linda did sleep while she was gone. At first Maggie spent her time looking through old magazines she found on the porch bookshelf. Becoming bored, and a little anxious, she went to the cradle and stared at Linda.

The baby's face seemed to be without a blemish, not a wrinkle save on its closed eyelids. Maggie stroked the fat cheek. It was like silk. Then she touched her own face. In comparison it seemed very rough. Was that what it was to grow older? Maggie asked herself.

For a while she concocted a brief story about a magical baby and its special powers. She soon tired of that and went back to the magazines. Finally she composed a postcard to her mother.

"Having a good time," she wrote. "The heat isn't so bad here at all. The lake is neat. There's a marsh, too. Love you a lot. Maggie."

After lunch there was a lot of preparation involved in bringing the baby to the beach and ocean swimming. Later on Maggie would figure out that it took more time going and returning than being there. Still, she and her father played in the surf, then took a walk along the water's edge in search of shells. As they walked she told him about some of the things she and Phyllis, her best friend in Seattle, had done. But even as she talked she sensed her father was not interested. He seemed preoccupied. Their walk was finished in silence.

When they returned to the cabin, Mr. Lavchek said he was going to take a nap. He suggested Maggie take one, too. "You must be bothered by jet lag," he said.

"I'm not."

"Well, I am," he said. It was clear he meant it as a joke, but no one laughed.

Maggie glanced around and saw Joanna's eyes on him. Instantly Maggie knew this tiredness, this nap, was a sign of her father's illness.

Maggie watched him as he went out to the lawn chair and very quickly fell asleep. The baby slept, too. Joanna sat on the porch reading a baby-care book.

Restless, Maggie slipped out of the cabin and made her way along the path through the trees. At the edge of the marsh she paused and looked out. Though brighter and warmer, it was as quiet as it had been that morning. She found a rock where she could sit and watch.

How long she sat there she was not sure. For a moment she thought she might even have dozed. In any case when she looked up, the heron was standing perfectly still in the water only twenty feet before her. Once again Maggie had the sensation that it had come by magical means. And once again, the beauty of the bird took her breath away.

Maggie gazed, rapt, as the heron began to move in its astonishingly slow way, lifting one stalklike leg at a time. Only once did Maggie see it make its lightning move to snap up something to eat.

As Maggie watched she recollected what her father had said about omens, in particular the kind of omen the heron was thought to be. Life *or* death. He made it sound as if she had to pick. But who would choose death? In any case—as far as Maggie was concerned—there was nothing deathlike about the heron. Except, perhaps, its grayness. Then she wondered if its way of suddenly disappearing was deathlike. The thought made her shudder. The more Maggie watched the heron, the more she began to speculate what it would be like if she could be as beautiful and graceful, calm and self-contained, as oblivious to the rest of the world as the heron seemingly was.

Gradually an idea formed in her mind: the heron would be her model. She would study it. Learn from it. Be it.

In midstep, the bird paused. It lifted its head, pointed its beak straight up, and called, "Frahnk! Frahnk!"

Maggie, wondering what had disturbed the bird, scrutinized the area carefully. Some seven feet beyond where the bird was standing—thirty feet from the shore—was one of the marsh's small, overgrown islands. This one was covered with bushes and one tree rose from its middle. The tree was dead.

Maggie looked at the island closely. For just a moment she thought she saw something blue moving among the bushes. The next moment she was distracted when the heron leaped into the air and flew away.

Quickly, she turned back to the island. Whatever was on the island—if anything was there—was no longer to be seen.

Over the next few days life at the cabin fell into a routine. Since Maggie was up early—secretly watching the heron—she took on the task of making breakfasts. Everyone made their own lunches. Maggie and Joanna did the dinners. Mr. Lavchek cleaned up after. Usually Maggie helped.

As for the baby, to Maggie it seemed to do very little other than eat and sleep, with occasional time to stare at the world, nurse, throw up, smile, and belch, not in any particular order and often in combinations. Joanna took complete charge of her. For Maggie, what was interesting was not the baby so much as Joanna's concentration, her involvement, her way of gazing at Linda.

"You like to look at her, don't you?" Maggie said to her one morning.

Joanna smiled. "I'm fascinated by how complex she is."

Maggie was surprised. "Is she complicated?"

"Oh, yes. Very. And more so every day."

Maggie studied Linda's face. The guileless eyes, the fat cheeks, the wet mouth, the tiny, fluttering breath— she did not seem complex to Maggie at all. Just the opposite. Very simple. "I guess I don't see it," Maggie confessed.

Joanna sighed, "Well, it's easier that way."

"What's easier?"

Joanna, caught up by her own remark, thought for a moment in search of an explanation. She said, "I guess everything is complicated. But if you had to look at the world that way, well, you'd be exhausted, wouldn't you? So you have to decide for yourself: What do I want to be simple? What do I want to be complicated?"

"Can you decide a thing like that?"

Joanna smiled wistfully. "I'm not sure," she replied.

"Even though you believe it?"

"Even though," Joanna admitted.

It was Mr. Lavchek's activities, his reading of papers, the constant calls he received or made, that set the tone for their days. There were times he would brook no interruptions at all but fuss and fume that the summer was running away from him like an untamed horse, that he was not getting done what he had to do. Not that he was very specific. It was all very vague. Even the calls taken on his portable phone were made in corners or on the lawn, always private, always intense. At other times he would take over the porch table or set himself up in the lawn chair, surrounding himself with files and papers, crouching down behind the wall he'd constructed. The silence was breached only by the occasional turn of a page, the murmur of his phone voice.

But once, when Maggie went by him—he had been working out on the lawn—she realized he was only sleeping. His mouth was open. His breathing was labored. He looked old.

There were times, however, when he would spring up from his work, scattering papers, and insist, almost in a rage, that Maggie was not doing anything worthy of a vacation. "Come on! Come on!" he would call. "Let's get our money's worth! Let's go swimming!" Or it would be the canoe. Or an expedition to a store or the beach. Those times, full of frantic energy, were more like Maggie's previous August visits. But inevitably, Mr. Lavchek would soon start glancing at his watch and begin to say, "I should be home." And it was not long before they would be.

In fact, Maggie and her father did not talk very much. But she was not that interested in his endless lectures about the state of the economy (bad), politicians (corrupt), business (unethical) . . . lectures that were meaningless to her and to which she listened, at best, listlessly. Very quickly, too, she decided he was not concerned about what she had to say about her life in Seattle. Even as she came to that conclusion—they were walking on the beach—he said, "I get a real pleasure listening to you talk."

"You do?"

"I like kids."

"You don't pay much attention to Linda."

"Maggie, I'm trying to spend time with you. Anyway, kids don't get interesting until they are five or six."

"How old was I when you left Mom?"

Her father did not answer right away. When he did speak he was petulant. "I didn't *leave* your mother. We split by mutual consent. And I don't remember how old you were."

"Six."

Her father frowned but said nothing.

Evenings they sat about in the little cabin. There was no television and what was available on the radio did not hold anyone's attention for long.

Mr. Lavchek, sometimes restless, was all for playing games. Board games. Cards. He liked to win, though he praised Maggie highly when she won. He announced he was going to learn chess but, after buying a chess set and an instruction book, quickly gave it up. Maggie reread her three favorite books, *A Wrinkle in Time, The Wizard of Oz*, and *Ancient Tales of Magic*, with the wonderfully interlocked adventures of Greek and Roman gods and goddesses. As for Joanna, she seemed to have an endless supply of books about motherhood and babies.

All during this time, thoughts about the heron were never totally absent from Maggie's mind. It was a kind of game she played. "If I were the heron," she would ask herself, "how would I drink this glass of milk?" Or, "If I were the heron, how would I walk from the porch to the edge of the lake?"

Once her father, exasperated, said, "For God's sake, Maggie, you seem positively locked in slow motion!"

Maggie took it—privately—as a compliment.

Each night, before going to sleep, Maggie set her travel alarm clock for six-thirty in the morning and placed it under her pillow. The soft tinkling sound called her without waking anyone else. For a few moments she would gaze at the crystal dangling overhead. It put her, she thought, in a magic mood. Then, barefooted, in her nightgown—with a sweater pulled over against the chill—she crept down from her loft and walked, never ran, along the cool path between the sap-oozing trees until she reached the rock. There she sat, deliciously cool, watching, waiting, as the morning's white mist eddied over the marsh. The thought that she was doing this secretly added much to her pleasure. It was Maggie's special time.

Often the heron was already there—as if waiting for her. At least Maggie liked to think that was the case. There were times, however, either when the heron never appeared or when Maggie had to wait for it to arrive. She actually liked the waiting time best. For then, when the great bird did come, it seemed to just *appear*, like a ghost, a spirit, a fairy.

Sometimes Maggie wished that the bird was not real. Instead, she conjured up notions that it was a transformed god—it happened all the time in the old myths. It did not really matter who or what god. She told herself stories about how she might release it from its heron shape.

As for the heron, it never appeared to notice Maggie but went about searching for food in its slow, magisterial way. But once, when Maggie's foot slipped and made a scraping noise against the rock, the bird instantly lifted its head straight up and gave its call, "Frahnk!" Maggie had come to understand the gesture and the call as a warning, a note of distress. This time though, the bird did something else. It turned and looked straight at Maggie.

Maggie held her breath. She could feel the bird's lemon-colored eyes staring right at her. Heart beating, she stared back. Surely now, if the magic books, the myths, were true, *something* would be revealed. But the heron did nothing. Absolutely nothing. It simply looked back into the water and went on with its search for food.

Most late afternoons—just before the time for getting dinner ready—Maggie returned to the marsh and "her" rock, as she called it. There she'd perch, book in hand, intending to read. In fact, she was looking for the heron. When it did come—if it came—Maggie watched it for an hour. She saw it had its favorite places. Its favorite walks. She came to believe she could see differences in its moods, judging it to be more serene one day, more agitated another. Over time she gradually began to realize that the small bush-covered island was near a place the heron liked to fish. That same area, however, also made it particularly nervous. Maggie took to wondering why.

CHAPTER

10

After five days of watching the heron, Maggie realized that the way the bird walked in search of food was not—as she first had thought—purely random. The bird followed a certain route.

First, the heron traveled from Maggie's right to her left. Then the bird moved from shallow to deeper water—though it never moved to any deep place. Nor did it go in a straight line. Instead it walked in zigzag fashion toward one particular island.

The island, like many in the marsh, was not very big and was covered with thick bushes. It was the same island on which Maggie had once seen—or thought she had seen—a patch of blue. The island's one distinguishing feature was the leafless tree that rose up from its center. It made Maggie think of a skeleton's shadow.

The heron would approach this island only to withdraw, approach, then withdraw, acting as if nervous about something. Frequently, when it drew near, it lifted its head, beak pointing skyward, and acted as if it were listening. More than once it gave its call, "Frahnk!" Any number of times it even flew abruptly away. Maggie never could tell why.

All the same, Maggie noticed that when the heron did reach a certain area, a place about five or six feet from the island, it plunged its head down more often than elsewhere. It seemed to feed with great success there. Clearly then, it wanted to be in that place, and yet, it was always unusually cautious.

Maggie decided that she needed to know why.

That evening at dinner she asked, "Are there any wild animals in these woods?"

"I should think," her father replied. "Mice. Chipmunks. Squirrels."

"What about big animals?"

"Is a rabbit big?" Joanna asked.

"Compared to a mouse," Maggie said, laughing.

"What about deer?" Joanna added. "Though I haven't seen one."

Mr. Lavchek nodded. "And raccoons. Woodchucks. Fox."

"All those?" Maggie cried, surprised.

"Plus wildcats. They all move around at night," her father said. "To avoid people."

"Would, would . . . any of them," Maggie asked, "be in the swamp?"

"What do you mean?"

"You know, could they swim?"

"All mammals can swim. Even cats, though they don't like to."

"No. I mean, would any of them go onto one of those islands in the marsh and, you know, try fishing, or try to catch the . . . heron?"

"The fox is notorious for killing chickens," her father told her. "But a heron is far too big for a fox. A duck, perhaps. Canada goose, maybe, though I doubt it. But no, not the heron. What makes you ask?"

"Just curious," Maggie said. Their answers had not satisfied her.

The following morning—it was Maggie's seventh day, just one week after her arrival at Sawdy Pond—when she slipped away to the marsh for her dawn watch of the heron, it did not appear. Not at all. After breakfast she took the canoe onto the lake and headed for the marsh.

The lake breeze was down. The air was hot and sticky. Overhead the sky was a brilliant blue, though off to the west great piles of clouds were beginning to build. Her father had said something about rain. But besides the clouds, nothing seemed to be moving except the occasional darting dragonfly.

The dragonfly, she could hear her father telling her,

has been around for three hundred and fifty million years. It can fly ninety miles an hour and has fifteen thousand lenses in its eyes. What's more, dragonflies eat twice their weight in mosquitoes each hour.

Maggie thought about these facts. She liked knowing them. Why did she find it annoying when her father told them to her? Because his knowing a fact seemed more important than the fact itself? Was it his method of getting her to stop thinking of magic? She did not know. What she did sense was that something was wrong with her father. Just as there was something not right with him and Joanna. Was it the baby? His heart? Something else? Whatever it was, it was upsetting.

Maggie paddled on. As she guided the canoe through the channel and into the marsh, the only noise was the quiet splash of her paddle. She was going slowly. As the marsh opened before her, the stillness had a calming effect.

For a moment she held the canoe in place so as to orient herself. Automatically she searched for the heron. It was the island, though—the one that caused the heron to be so cautious—that she wanted to find. Off to the right she thought she saw the rock where she sat. She aimed for it.

The canoe slid over the water lilies with a slight hiss. Now and again she looked down into the shallow water. A few fish flitted by. There were ancient logs beneath the water, too, twisted and knurled, like misshapen fists.

She approached her rock. She could see her path and,

through the trees, the obscure outline of their cabin. She turned the canoe, about to make certain where the island was. Made distinct by the dead tree, it stood some thirty feet from the shore. She aimed the canoe right at it.

The water beneath her was shallow. Maggie realized she probably could have walked the entire distance. Reminding herself that the bottom might be oozy, she was glad she was going this way.

The prow of the canoe bumped against the island. She studied the bit of land for a while but could see nothing that might cause the bird—or her—concern.

She scrambled to the bow of the canoe, then stepped carefully onto the shore. The island's edge was soft, matted with grass, but strong enough to hold her. She pulled the canoe up and made it secure.

Maggie had approached the island from the side nearest their cabin, just opposite where she always sat on her rock. When she turned she could see her rock very clearly. She realized the heron, from its favorite place in the water right off the island, had to be seeing her with equal clarity. Yet, save for that one time, the bird had not appeared to notice her.

Maggie tried to imagine what the heron thought of her. Wouldn't it be neat if it could read *her* thoughts? Did the heron know she wanted to look, admire, and learn from it? Smiling at her own whimsy, Maggie turned to the task of exploring the tiny island.

The island was no more, Maggie guessed, than fifteen or twenty feet across, and completely overgrown with bushes. The bushes, now that she saw them up close, were taller than she had thought. And, though most of the berries were gone, they were berry bushes. Here and there a few remained. Blackberries.

Maggie pushed her hand amongst the leaves and felt a prick of pain. Only then did she discover the bushes were covered with sharp brambles. Quickly, she withdrew her hand and found that she had scratched herself, drawing blood. When she reached in again she took greater care. A berry dropped off into her hand. It tasted wonderfully sweet. She examined her hand. Her fingers were now stained by berry juice as well as blood.

She gazed up at the dead tree that rose from the middle of the island. Perhaps it was not just the heron that meant two things. Maybe everything about the marsh was about life. And death.

Deciding that she would think about that later, Maggie continued her exploration. The bushes were so thick she could not go through them. To get anywhere, she had to move along the edge of the island, taking care of her footing. Now and again she paused to get some berries and eat them.

When she got to the other side of the island, opposite where she had landed, she made her first discovery. She found something very much like a passageway into the brambles, a passageway that seemed to lead right into the interior of the island.

Something about the passageway—it did not appear natural but more as though it been cut through, like a tunnel—made her study it with greater care. The ground, she saw, was smooth—as though often used.

Her curiosity growing, Maggie moved into the tunnel. After three steps she was surrounded by bushes. First she had to stoop, then finally, to crawl forward. When she reached the end, she found herself in a space that was like a cave hollowed out in the middle of the bushes. These bushes even rose overhead and made a lacy ceiling. In the center was the trunk of the dead tree. The ground was well trampled, with space enough to sit, even to lie down.

At first she was charmed. It was wonderfully snug.

Her first notion was that it was a nest. But if it were a nest, she reminded herself, it would have to be for some gigantic bird or animal. That, she told herself, was not likely. Unless, she allowed herself the thought, it was some fantastic creature.

No, whatever the space was, it was not natural. It could not have grown this way. Somebody—or thing—had made the place. For what purpose? Maggie kept asking herself.

After poking around for a while Maggie discovered—set into the bushes as though hidden—a long wooden box. The lid was hinged. She lifted it cautiously.

Inside were some comic books, a chipped mug, and some saltine crackers wrapped in plastic. There was an envelope, too, a jar of peanut butter, and a tiny radio, cracked, with an earpiece. But what riveted Maggie's attention was a bow with a quiver of arrows.

Maggie stared at the bow and arrows for a long time. Cautiously, she reached down and touched a finger to one of the arrowheads. It was sharp.

Almost instantly, Maggie recalled the patch of blue she had seen on the island. It must have been some person. She remembered, too, the sense of unease the heron exhibited whenever he drew near the island.

Maggie picked up the envelope and looked at it. In the upper left corner it read, "Westport School District. John F. Kennedy School." Handwritten were the words "Mr. and Mrs. St. Claire."

After a moment of hesitation, Maggie opened the

envelope. It was a school form, torn in two. Maggie held them together and read the words:

> To: *Mr. and Mrs. St. Claire*
> From: *Ms. E. Kirk*
> Re: *Tucker*
> *Please call and make an appointment to see me regarding your son. I'm afraid he's still causing problems, being the bully, provoking fights, bad language, etc.*

Suddenly aware that this was none of her business, Maggie quickly put the torn paper back into the envelope, returned it to the box, shut the lid, and placed the box where it had been. Then she scrambled back along the bramble passage and made her way around to the canoe. Once in it she paddled hastily out of the marsh. Only when she got out on the lake did she begin to calm down.

There, she forced herself to think about what she had seen. That somebody had been on that island—used it—was perfectly clear. She thought about the note. It suggested the kind of person who was there. This "Tucker"—if that's who it was—did not seem very nice. A "bully," the note said. And the bow and arrows—sharp arrows—suggested violence. She wondered how old Tucker was. And she would have bet anything he had not brought the note to his parents. He had hidden it.

Suddenly a whole new idea came to her: Maybe this Tucker was trying to kill the heron. The thought was enough to make Maggie ill.

Maggie turned the canoe around and thought about going back into the marsh. Instead, she decided it would be better if she watched from her place. Only then did it occur to her that even as she was watching the heron, maybe someone had been watching *her*.

CHAPTER

12

 *When Maggie got back* to their dock, her father was on the lawn talking on the phone. Joanna was on the porch playing with the baby, who lay in her cradle.

"Maggie," she called, "look!"

Joanna was holding a rattle over Linda, shaking it. Each time she did, the baby burst into a smile and gurgled, waving her arms and legs. It made Joanna laugh.

Maggie came to Joanna's side and looked down.

"Isn't it wonderful?" Joanna said. "Just a few days ago she wasn't doing that."

"Doing what?"

"That kind of response. She suddenly seems to be able to focus in a new way. She's beginning to see the world. Connect with it. Come alive!" She shook the rattle and again Linda reacted.

"It's so weird to think," Joanna said, serious now, "that we were all this way, once. I mean, *everyone*. Can you imagine your father like this?" She giggled.

Maggie laughed, too. The image did seem absurd.

"It's really amazing," Joanna went on. "Just think, you have to learn almost *everything*." She put aside the rattle, scooped Linda up, and covered her face with wet kisses. "I never knew I could love anyone so much."

Maggie smiled but said nothing. And even as she watched she saw a change come over Joanna's face. It had become sad. Then, to Maggie's astonishment, a tear trickled down Joanna's face.

"What is it?" Maggie asked.

"Oh, Maggie. It's so hard!" Joanna's voice came out as a whisper.

"What's so hard?" Maggie replied, bewildered.

Joanna turned around to face her. Maggie saw what seemed a wild look. "Everything . . ."

Swinging away from Maggie, Joanna went out on the lawn with the baby enfolded in her arms.

Maggie watched Joanna move toward her father, who, papers on his lap, was on the phone. When Joanna reached him she paused briefly but said nothing, only looked down. After a moment, when Maggie's father did not look up, Joanna continued on down toward the lakefront. There she stood, gazing over the water.

A sudden headache made Maggie want an aspirin. She went into the toilet room. Over the little sink was a mirrored medicine chest. She stared at her own face. Her face was round, like her father's. But she had her mother's chestnut hair. And her mother's eyes. Her mouth, she decided, was her own. If I were the heron, Maggie asked herself, how would I hold my head?

She lifted her chin, trying to stretch her neck. Then she turned slightly, viewing herself from an angle.

Suddenly feeling silly, she pulled back the mirror and searched for aspirin. She was about to reach for it when she saw three medicine containers. In a glance she saw that they were her father's medicine.

She picked one off the shelf and read the instructions. "A. Lavchek. 1 pill to be taken 3 times daily after meals." It was dated almost a month ago.

Maggie shook the jar. It made no noise. Puzzled, she tried to undo the top. When it failed to move, she realized it was a childproof cap. Deftly, she pushed down, then twisted. The top came off. She looked in. The neck was covered with foil. She plucked at it. The container was still sealed. She could see the cotton packing, and the jar was full of capsules.

Maggie checked the other two containers. Each had been prescribed on the same date. Though dosages were different, he was supposed to take them every day. But the evidence was equally clear: her father was not taking any of his medicine.

Slowly, Maggie put the containers back, then wandered out onto the porch. Joanna was sitting by the water. From the way she was sitting, Maggie could tell she was nursing the baby.

She looked at her father. His book had slipped to the ground. His arm and hand hung to one side. Maggie's heart gave a frightened leap. She rushed out and went to his side.

"Dad!" she called.

He started and opened his eyes. "What's that, kid?"

"I thought . . ."

"You thought what?"

"Nothing . . ."

"Hey, kid, I was having a sweet snooze."

"Sorry . . ." Maggie started to walk back toward the cabin. Suddenly she heard, "Frahnk!" She froze where she stood and listened.

"Frahnk!"

It was the heron's warning call. Maggie began to run.

CHAPTER
13

Breathless, Maggie reached her rock. From there she gazed in every direction. The heron was nowhere to be seen. Finally she turned to the island and examined it. There was not the slightest hint that anything was amiss.

Yet the heron *had* been there. Maggie was certain of it. She had heard its agitated call, a call that meant it had been disturbed or—it certainly sounded that way— threatened. It was as if the heron had been calling *her*. But now, nothing. Where *was* it? An urgency, made painful by helplessness, took hold of Maggie.

Weary, upset, she sank down on her rock and wrapped her hands around her knees, clasped her fingers tightly, and stared out over the water. Everything appeared to be completely calm. It was she who was agitated.

The more she sat there, however, the more she realized that to hear *nothing* was in itself unnatural. No dragonflies teased the air. No shrill "kouk-la-ree" from red-winged blackbirds. Even the marsh waters were placid. It was, she suddenly realized, as if everything was being held in a state of suspense.

With growing unease Maggie once again examined the area for some sign of the heron. This time she caught sight of a feather floating idly in the water. For a moment she just stared at it. When she grasped the fact that the feather's color was gray-blue, her heart seemed to squeeze.

Maggie wasted no time. Kicking off her sneakers, she jumped off her rock, moved from the mossy bank, and stepped into the water. The moment she did she sank ankle-deep into oozing mud. Unsteady, not sure if she should take the risk of going any farther, she kept her eyes on the feather as if to will it toward her. It did not come.

Maggie attempted another step. This time she struck a firmer bottom. Encouraged, she moved ahead a few inches. Though the water became deeper, the bottom continued to hold. For a while all was fine. She had covered a quarter of the distance from the shore to the island. The water was above her knees. Then, unexpectedly, she struck a soft spot and sank almost a foot. It frightened her but she held firm. Allowing herself to rest for a moment, Maggie looked about for the feather. It was still there, still out of reach, tossing gently in the waves she herself had made. She realized that if she had thought to bring a stick she might have been able to reach it. Annoyed at herself for not thinking, she looked quickly about for something that could help.

About four feet from where she stood, she caught sight of a slender stick floating just below the surface of the water. Certain that with the stick she could get the feather, she struggled a bit farther, leaned out, and was just about to take hold of the stick when she realized that it was an arrow. Her hand froze.

The next moment Maggie was all energy. No longer caring where she stepped, she pulled up her leg with brute strength. Floundering in her struggle for firmer footing, she slogged toward the arrow and grabbed it. A quick examination left no doubt: The arrow was from the island.

Maggie swiveled about to look at the feather. Little need then to *guess* what had happened. Someone on the island had taken a shot at the heron. The arrow had come close—the feather was proof of that—but, hopefully, no more.

Maggie forced herself to acknowledge that there was no evidence to prove the person had missed the heron. Perhaps the person had killed it and dragged it away. Yet, even as she stood there, arrow in her hand, Maggie did not think that was what had happened. After all, she was *holding* the arrow. It had not gone into the bird. Just the thought of such a thing, though, made her feel weak.

Grasping the arrow firmly, Maggie struggled back to shore and climbed onto her rock. Her legs were dripping with bad-smelling mud. She was exhausted. All the same she was determined to wait until she saw or heard some sign—any sign—that the heron was still alive.

Maggie's breath and heartbeat gradually returned to normal. More calmly now, she began to think, trying to figure out why anyone would want to kill the heron. She considered target practice, a desire to have the bird's feathers. . . . But there was—she knew—no way of knowing. The only sure thing was that it had been someone who cared nothing for the bird.

But how, she wondered, could that *be*, when the bird was so beautiful? Still, the evidence was clear: The hunter had taken time to construct a hiding place, then watched and waited. It was someone with a lot of patience and skill as well as cunning.

Maggie tried to recall kids she knew back home who might do such a thing. There were mean ones, bullies in her school, but even they—she was positive—would not want to kill the heron. It was too cruel. No, she could not contemplate such a person.

Then Maggie asked herself if there was any connection between her going to the island and the shooting. Was it just a coincidence? Or had one led to the other?

It was almost as though someone was telling her she *was* being watched.

Weary, Maggie bowed her head, burrowed it into her arms, closed her eyes, and let her mind drift. She thought about her home in Seattle. Her mother. Her own trip East. It was not long before she came around to recalling her discovery regarding her father, that he was not taking his medicine.

Suddenly, as though a stout wall had been breached, she confronted the whole problem of her father. Why hadn't he met her at the plane? Why was he so moody? Why was there so much tension with Joanna? What about his apparent disinterest in the baby? Finally, and the most dangerous thing of all, why was he not taking his medicine, medicine that Joanna had said he needed? *What was the matter with him?*

Maggie heard a slight sound. She lifted her head. The heron was standing right before her in the shallows. It was very still, gazing into the water in search of food as if nothing at all had happened.

Maggie's heart swelled. It *had* called to her, asking her for protection. Perhaps she had even given it. She barely wondered at the love she felt for the bird. How she longed to protect it! Keep it from harm. If only she had real magic!

Maggie made a decision. Magic or no, she would do everything to protect the heron. As though to signal the heron to witness this decision, she held up the arrow with two hands and broke it across a knee, then flung the bits into the woods behind her.

The bird swung its head to stare in her direction, then went on with its grazing.

Maggie got up. Her action made her feel a little less helpless. Glancing one last time over her shoulder at the heron, she walked back to the cabin.

CHAPTER

14

That night, after dinner and cleanup, Joanna was putting Linda to bed when she said, "Maggie, want to take a walk?"

"Might rain," Mr. Lavchek announced from across the room, where he was reading papers.

"We can cover up," Joanna said. She looked to Maggie again. "How about it?"

Maggie, certain Joanna wanted to talk to her about her afternoon tears, only knew she did not want to go.

"Please . . ." Joanna said.

The pleading tone in her voice gave Maggie no choice. "Okay," she said, trying to smile.

"Cover yourselves," her father said, without looking up from his reading.

It was humid outside. Above they could see neither

moon nor stars. Looking toward the lake, Maggie saw flashes in the sky, then heard the distant rumble of thunder.

"Rain's coming," Maggie said.

"We won't go far."

Joanna, not saying any more, guided them along the dirt road that led from the cabin. She had brought a flashlight, which she aimed at the road so they might avoid rocks and ruts. Otherwise it was pitch-dark.

Now and again the thunder came. It was drawing closer. Occasionally Maggie looked ahead, where she knew Joanna was. She could not see her face. Maggie wondered if the darkness was the reason Joanna had suggested the walk.

They had gone about a quarter of a mile when Joanna said, "I'm sorry I got so upset this afternoon."

"That's all right," Maggie said.

"Well, it's supposed to be your vacation. And ours. Actually, this is the first time since I've known your father that he's taken a real vacation. You know, three days, a week at most. He said he wanted a real family time. Well, you can see for yourself how uncomfortable he is with it."

They continued to walk in silence. Maggie listened to the sounds of their feet crunching on the ground gravel, the grinding chirp of crickets.

Then Joanna said, "Taking care of the baby . . . You can see how much I love her, can't you?"

"Yes," Maggie assured her.

"Well, all the same . . ." Joanna took a deep breath. "It's just that sometimes . . . it gets overwhelming." Now each word sounded painful. "I honestly never imagined it would be so hard. And I'm afraid your father doesn't get involved very much."

"I know," Maggie said sympathetically. She had a feeling of pride that Joanna would talk to her this way. But she still was fearful that she was about to be told something she would not want to know.

Hearing Joanna sigh, Maggie stopped. Joanna stopped, too. Maggie was sure Joanna was trying to say something so difficult it was hard to get it out. She wished she could help her but did not know how.

"There are times . . ." Joanna began, only to falter. "Times," she began anew, "times I—hate the baby." The moment the words were said, Joanna began to weep quietly.

Maggie, not knowing what else to do, reached out and touched Joanna's arm. Joanna grasped her hand and squeezed it.

"I'm sorry," Joanna said between sobs. "This is not fair to you. I just needed to say it. Say it out loud."

"That's okay," Maggie said, though she did not know what she felt. What Joanna said sounded awful.

"But it's true," Joanna now rushed on. "The baby is so innocent but demands so much of me! So much there's nothing left. I get to feel so resentful. Then the next moment I'm ashamed to feel that way. And your father . . . well, you see it, don't you? He's sick. And he's upset. I don't know why. And he gets angry at me. There are times I think he's jealous of the baby. So we're having a hard time. At the *worst* time. I can't get angry at the baby. And I try not to get angry at your father. But I do. . . ."

Joanna reached out and compulsively drew Maggie to her, hugging her hard, even as she wept. "Is all this stupid?" she managed to say.

"No," Maggie replied, though her head was in a whirl. She hardly knew what to make of the things Joanna was saying.

"If there were only some reason . . ." Joanna went on. "Oh, Maggie, I'm so glad you're here," Joanna said. *"So glad!"* She released Maggie.

"Joanna . . ." Maggie said, suddenly remembering something.

"What?"

"Maybe Dad's acting this way because he isn't taking his medicine."

Maggie heard Joanna catch her breath. "What do you mean?"

"I was looking for aspirin in the medicine cabinet," Maggie explained. "And I saw the bottles with the stuff he's supposed to take. I don't know why but I looked. He never opened them."

Joanna uttered a small moan. For a long time they just stood there.

"Maggie," Joanna said softly.

"What?"

"Would you speak to him?"

"About what?"

"The medicine. I can't. I just know he'll blow up at me. It would be the last straw. Would you?"

Maggie, feeling trapped, said, "I'll try."

Joanna reached out and hugged Maggie again. "I told you how glad I am you're here," she whispered. "I really am." A few raindrops began to fall.

By unspoken consent they turned about and walked back in silence, holding hands like sisters. Maggie kept wondering what she could say to her father or how, but she did not want to tell that to Joanna.

Just as they got to the cabin, Joanna gave Maggie another hug and said, "Thanks for letting me talk. I feel better. Maggie, honest now, do you think I'm a monster?"

"No," Maggie said instantly, for that was easy to say. As for what she *did* think, she was not so sure.

When they went inside they found that Mr. Lavchek had fallen asleep in his chair. Maggie, grateful for the reprieve, climbed up to her loft.

Once there she lay back in her bed. She stared at her crystal. The rain beat down on the roof. Thunder rumbled. Thoughts continued to flood in. The heron . . . Joanna . . . her father . . . in a way they were all asking her to help. Maggie gazed at her audience of magical creatures and people. If only they could help her. She knew they could not. Slowly, she picked them up and placed them in a corner of the loft. She would have to think about magic in a different kind of way.

She turned out her light but aimed her flashlight at the crystal. It seemed like her own star. Perhaps a wishing star. "Star bright, star light," she started to say, then stopped and turned off the flashlight.

In the darkness she listened to the rain. When it rained, where did the heron go? She imagined it on the marsh, moving slowly, ever so slowly. . . .

CHAPTER

15

 *It was about six-thirty* the following morning when Maggie's alarm—placed under her pillow—woke her. Wearing jeans and a sweater, barefooted, she ran across the wet lawn and at the water's edge stepped into the canoe. Kneeling, she pushed off from shore and allowed herself to glide out on the lake. The water was smooth as a mirror, as warm as flesh. The sun was a white hole in the gray mist. The only sound was the squawk of an invisible gull.

Slowly, Maggie paddled toward the channel and soon entered the marsh. Now the mist clung as the sun all but disappeared. Her hair became damp. Droplets of water trickled down her face. She could not see far. A red-winged blackbird startled her with a near and sudden challenge: "Kouk-la-ree! Kouk-la-ree!"

As Maggie continued to glide forward, she passed dead trees as well as boulders sticking out of the water. The boulders, she decided, were hulking guard-beasts rising from watery beds to observe her arrival in this no-man's-land. The black and leafless trees were captured souls of unwelcome intruders.

Once Maggie sensed she had reached the middle of the marsh, she stopped paddling and rested the paddle across her knees. Though she could barely see more than five feet in any direction, she looked back over her shoulder and tried to determine just where she had entered the marsh. Then she moved slowly to the right, hoping she had aimed correctly. She wanted to get close to where the heron fed.

More than once Maggie bumped into a little island or a partially submerged and blackened stump. Each time she backed off but continued to probe her way forward. Every few moments she stopped and listened to the swollen stillness. From far away a rooster crowed just as he had during her first morning at the lake. But here on the marsh, day had yet to come.

It was while pausing and listening that Maggie heard something she had not heard before. It was a slow, regular, *slip-slop, slip-slop* sound. What first came to mind was someone scooping up water. Knowing how improbable that was, Maggie concentrated harder. It did not take long before she decided that the sound was very much like the noise she had been making, that of someone paddling. Her heart began to race. She was not the only one on the marsh.

Afraid to move and give herself away, Maggie attempted to stare through the mist. It was too thick to see anything. Then she strained to determine the exact direction of the sound. She guessed that it was coming from somewhere in front of her and to the left.

With great care Maggie lowered her paddle into the water. Her canoe slid forward silently. Then she drifted and listened.

Once again she heard the sound of the other paddler. This time the sound was closer. And it was moving in her direction.

Holding her breath with nervous excitement, Maggie stared into the mist toward where she thought the sound was coming from. Sure enough, through the swirling gray, she began to make out a lumpish, yellow shape. It sat low and wide in the water and moved forward in short jerks. Heart thumping, Maggie strained to see more. The thing, whatever it was, loomed larger with every jerk. Now she saw: It was some kind of boat. And sitting in its middle was what appeared to be a small, bent figure lurching clumsily back and forth.

Maggie held her breath. The figure in the boat turned toward her. Momentarily Maggie saw the blur of a white, ghostlike face. Suddenly she recalled the Greek myth of Charon, the ghostly ferryman who conveyed the souls of the dead across the river Styx. Her neck prickled with fear. Even so, she continued to gaze into the mist, full of the sensation that she was in a horror movie but watching it, too. Then, recalling herself to reality and wanting to get closer, she touched her paddle to the water and gave a hard pull. With a thud, she bumped into an island. Taken by surprise, she dropped her paddle with a splash. Frightened by the sound, Maggie twisted about and snatched the paddle out of the water. Turning, she scrutinized the area where she had seen the boat and rower. Both had gone.

Maggie listened hard. The sound was gone, too. The rower must have heard her and been frightened off. Or perhaps, he was simply hiding in the mist, listening for her. Waiting for her.

Maggie, trying to decide what to do, let her canoe drift aimlessly. Then, with a start, she realized that the person she'd seen might well be going where the heron was. It was urgent she get there, too.

Maggie looked up and around. She was not sure where she was. She must be patient. Gradually the mist became thinner, allowing her to see a greater distance. As the disk of sun moved higher into the sky, it grew more brilliant. Still, she found it impossible to place herself in the marsh with any precision.

Too impatient to wait more and no longer caring if she made noise, Maggie paddled until she could make out a shoreline. By keeping close to the water's edge, she continued to move in search of some clue that would tell her just where she was.

Moment by moment the air grew brighter. More than

once she spied rocks on the shore and thought them *her* rock. Each time, however, when she drew closer it proved not so. She paddled faster. She found yet another rock. This one looked more promising. The more she studied it, the more certain she grew that it was the right one. Pleased with herself, she aimed for the shore, reached it, and hopped out of the canoe.

She ran to the rock. Yes, she had found it. Quickly, she turned and looked out over the marsh. Now she could see the island with enough clarity to be sure it, too, was the island she had been looking for.

Hurrying back to her canoe, she got in it, pushed out, and paddled toward the island. It took but moments to reach it. She edged around to the other side, where the passageway was.

Once more she listened. Once again, there was only silence. But silence in the marsh, Maggie reminded herself, meant that things were not right.

CHAPTER

16

Maggie got out, hauled her boat partly up onto the island, and without thinking a great deal about what she was doing, began to scramble down the passageway. It was gloomy, and the musty smell of damp ground and leaves was strong. Only while she was crawling forward did she decide she was making a mistake. She had no business being there. Not before and not this time. For a moment she remained motionless, trapped between fear and the desire to learn more.

More nervous than ever, she decided to inch forward, and before she had time to think about what or whom she might meet, she found herself in the open area. No one was there. Still, she could not free herself of the thought that the person she had seen was coming to this place.

With her eyes now accustomed to the gloom, she looked about. Almost immediately she noticed that the long box—the one that had contained the bow and arrows—had been pulled from its hiding place and was open. Bow and arrows were gone. So was the envelope from the school.

The person *had* already come there!

Not wanting to remain a moment longer, Maggie scrambled back along the passageway and was soon standing next to her canoe.

Even as she stood there she heard a splash off to her right. It seemed to come from the center of the marsh. She turned quickly, just in time to see a smudge of yellow drift out of view. The boat!

Maggie shoved the canoe back into the water and all but jumped into it. Then she whipped her paddle about and began to stroke hard, shooting out in pursuit of the yellow boat.

Five strokes and she caught another glimpse of her quarry. This time she saw the boat for what it truly was, a raft. And she could just begin to make out the person in it. He did not seem very big—hardly more than a kid.

Deciding it would be best to follow, Maggie let the raft continue on. It was moving in the jerky fashion she had first observed. She followed carefully.

Maggie was not certain but sensed that the raft-owner was going directly to the far side of the marsh. She kept behind the raft, more than once losing sight of it. But, pressing on, she would catch sight of it again.

Maggie had been paddling for about twenty minutes when she realized that the raft was no longer moving. Instead, she was gaining on it rapidly, faster than she wanted. Immediately she slowed down. The raft had reached the far side of the marsh. It was no longer in the water but being hauled up on land.

Dipping her paddle, Maggie slid the canoe forward cautiously. In moments she was just offshore. There was no dock. There was, however, a pathway leading from where the raft had been left through an avenue of trees. At the far end of the avenue she could make out a white house. It was considerably bigger than their cabin, more like a regular-sized house. Maggie was unable to see any signs of life.

As she continued to sit in the canoe, Maggie was uncertain what to do. She was tempted to move forward, get on the shore and explore. Then she remembered she was not at all sure who she might meet. In all likelihood it was that "Tucker."

Deciding she had better be a little more careful, Maggie turned the canoe about and headed back across and out of the marsh.

 *"Do you know* who lives in that house on the other side of the marsh?" Maggie asked during breakfast.

Her father was reading a business newspaper. Joanna was drinking a cup of skim milk while balancing Linda on her knee.

"I don't," Joanna said.

"What?" Mr. Lavchek said without looking up.

"Who lives on the other side of the marsh?" Maggie repeated.

Mr. Lavchek shook his head.

Maggie said, "I think I'll go find out."

"Why?" Mr. Lavchek asked.

"Just . . . curious."

"People around here like their privacy," he warned.

"I know. . . ." Maggie returned, though she did not know.

"Do we have any plans?" Joanna asked. She was looking at Maggie. Maggie sensed Joanna was waiting for her to make a suggestion, perhaps to find a time that she might talk to her father about the medicine.

"I've got a lot of reading to do," Mr. Lavchek informed them.

"We could go a bookstore," Maggie suggested. "I've run out of books to read."

"You read too fast," her father said.

"I like to."

"Page turners," Mr. Lavchek said. "The term tells you there's nothing on the page worth savoring."

"My librarian," Maggie retorted, "says a page turner means that you *care* about what's happening to the characters."

Mr. Lavchek made a snuffling noise that sounded vaguely negative.

"Tomorrow morning," Joanna said after a moment of silence, "I'm going to church."

Mr. Lavchek looked up from his paper. "She's gone all religious on me." There was a mocking tone to his voice.

"What church?" Maggie asked Joanna.

"Congregational."

"I've never been."

"Come," Joanna said. Then she added, "The building is special."

Before Maggie could reply, Mr. Lavchek put his newspaper down. "Okay, here it is," he announced. "Work this morning. Beach this afternoon. Work tonight."

"Do the women have the right to vote?" Joanna asked sarcastically.

"The women can do whatever they want," Mr. Lavchek returned, and pushed himself away from the table.

When he had gone, Maggie and Joanna exchanged silent looks. Then Joanna said, "If you'd like, I'll take you to a bookstore."

"Maybe later," Maggie said. "I'm going to find out about that house across the marsh."

"Just be sure you don't bother people, okay?" Joanna said.

"I won't." Maggie began to clear the dishes.

Joanna held her arm. "I checked his medicine. And you're right. He isn't taking any. Are you going to speak to him?"

"I'll try."

"When?" Joanna sounded anxious.

"Soon as I can."

"Thanks. Look out though, he's in one of his moods." Maggie made a tentative effort to move but Joanna continued to hold her.

"Do you know what I realized?" Joanna said. "Since I'm twenty-eight and you're almost thirteen, it means you and I are closer in age than I am to your father. Isn't that weird?"

Maggie looked into Joanna's face. She could not tell if this was something that Joanna was happy about or not. All she could see was a lot of pain. "I guess," she replied.

As soon as she finished the breakfast dishes, Maggie walked down to the marsh and her rock. Not for the first time did she wish she could talk to her mother about what was happening. But her mother was not there and talking on the phone from the cabin would be too difficult. Besides, she did not like to talk to her mother about her father. In the first place it made her feel uncomfortable. And she was never sure exactly how her mother felt. Maybe that was why *she* felt uncomfortable.

She looked around. The heron was not there. Maggie was not bothered. But she did wish she, Maggie, could come and go. Silently. On her own terms.

On her way back to the cottage, Maggie decided that she should think of the exploration of the house across the marsh as an adventure. The best would be if she could find the person—this "Tucker"—who shot at the bird and convince him not to. The worst that might happen would be she could be chased away. Either way she knew she'd feel much better knowing *something* about the people who lived there. What's more, she decided, this was the time to go.

"I'm going out in the canoe," she announced first to Joanna, then to her father. Joanna had simply smiled and murmured something about "have a good time."

Her father, however, took her hand and stared up at her from his lawn chair.

"How you doing, kid? This a good vacation?"

"Sure."

"That's what I like to hear; one hundred percent enthusiasm. What's the matter?"

Maggie looked down at him. "How old are you?" she asked.

"You're supposed to say, 'How *young* are you?' Why?"

"You need a shave," she replied.

He laughed. "That's my girl. How about a date? Monday night. Just you and me. We'll go off to a movie. This is not like us—not going once yet."

"What about Joanna?"

"Church with her. Movie with me." Mr. Lavchek offered a wink, then dropped Maggie's hand. "Yeah, well, I'll talk to her." He turned back to his reading.

Maggie stood over him for a moment, trying to get the courage to talk to him about the medicine. She could not get it out.

"See you later," she said, and went down to the canoe.

The day had become much warmer. The sun was bright. There was even a breeze that ruffled the lake, coming from the direction of the ocean. For a moment Maggie just gazed at the lake, marveling at its many moods. She wondered if she had as many and decided she probably did.

She was in the marsh in no time. But to actually move toward the house on the other side of the marsh took a different kind of energy. It took time—not to get there, but to decide she was really going to do it.

She would pull toward it only to stop, asking herself how she would proceed when she got there. She knew it was this "Tucker" she wanted to see. Without meaning to, she had begun to construct an image of what he was like. A high school student. Maybe not big—the glimpse she caught of him suggested he was not—but certainly strong. And ugly, for she was sure he would have a cruel, mean face. Somehow she dreaded that the most. All the same she told herself she did not want to reveal any apprehension no matter how old—or tough-looking—he was.

Thoughts of age made Maggie think about what Joanna had said—about *their* ages. She understood now that Joanna had been trying to say the two of them were allied, an alliance *against* her father. Or maybe, Maggie considered, it was an alliance *for* her father? She did not know. What she did know was that her father had—at least as far as his medicine was concerned—become *her* responsibility. But why did it have to be her? The whole business made her uneasy.

With a shake of her head she looked at the yellow raft that lay on the lawn before her. New doubts sprang up about what she was doing. Perhaps she should put it off for another time. Then—with a start—she realized that it would not be so long before she had to return to Seattle. Once that happened there would be no way to protect the heron. Maggie gripped the paddle and began to move forward.

A few strokes brought her bumping against the shore. Before her Maggie saw a large expanse of lawn and trees. As for the house—as she had surmised before—it was much more than a summer place.

At first Maggie remained in the canoe and simply stared at the building, trying to read its character. It was long and low, its aluminum siding a fading yellow in color. Black shutters—she could see they were not working ones—were attached to every window. On the side of the house she was facing was a long deck. A screen door opened onto it but there was no sign of life.

In fact there was little indication that people were living in the house at all. On the deck was a chaise lounge and next to that was a bare table. The table had a round green awning shading it. Leaning against the deck there was a young person's bicycle. And of course, there was the raft.

Maggie stepped on the shore. After hauling the canoe up she turned toward the house, trying to quell her own nervousness. Slowly, she walked up the well-trimmed lawn. As she walked she could not free herself of the sensation that the house had been abandoned. A ghost house.

"Hello!" she called. When no answer came, she called again, louder. She went up the gray wooden steps to the deck. This time she heard voices come from inside.

"Hello!" she cried for a third time, trying to make up her mind what to do if no one answered. This time, however, the screen door opened. It was a boy.

Maggie judged him somewhat younger than she was, not much more than eleven. He was not very tall, his hair was blond, and his face was almost milky white. His face showed no emotion at all. None.

For a moment they just looked at each other.

"What do you want?" he asked her. The light made him squint.

"I . . . I live across the way," Maggie said. "The other side of the marsh."

"Yeah." His tone suggested he knew.

"Does . . . Tucker live here?" Maggie asked.

Instead of answering the boy said, "What's your name?"

"Maggie."

"What kind of name is that?"

"Short for Margaret."

"Yeah, well, I'm Tucker."

Maggie, surprised, just stared at him.

"That your canoe?" Tucker asked, looking past her.

"It belongs to the house we're staying at. Is that your raft?"

"My father's." Tucker squinted at her some more. "What did you want to see me about?" he asked.

Maggie hesitated.

"Want to come in? I'm the only one home," Tucker said. "I'm watching television."

Maggie nodded and stepped into a large room. Coming in from the bright sunlight made it seem dark. But she could tell it was kind of a living room. The only real light came from across the room where a large television was on. The neonlike colors of a cartoon flickered and danced. The music blared. Characters screamed at one another. Laughter erupted like automatic gunfire.

Tucker shut the door behind them. Without another word he brushed past Maggie and plopped himself down on the rug, rolled over on his stomach, propped his chin up with his hands, and stared at the screen.

Maggie remained by the door and looked around. She could see now that the room was fully carpeted and had a few pieces of bulky furniture. The television was at one end, while an elaborate fireplace was at the other end. It looked unused. Right over the fireplace was what appeared to be a mounted antique rifle. A coffee table carried carefully stacked magazines. Over the couch, on the wall, was a large framed color photo of a nature scene, a snowcapped mountain looming in the distance. On another wall was a group of framed photos of people. They were all smiling.

"Don't you want to watch?" Tucker said.

"A bit," Maggie answered. She sat down on the couch.

"Don't mess up the pillows," Tucker said without looking around. "My mother doesn't like it."

"I won't."

"You live in Finn's Lodge?"

Maggie remembered the name of the cabin. "Just for August. I'm visiting my father."

"What about your mother?"

"She lives in Seattle, Washington. I live with her."

"We live here all year round," Tucker said. "My father works in New Bedford. My mother works in Fall River."

Maggie looked around, almost expecting them to appear.

"They work Saturdays," Tucker said, as if reading her mind. "I'm at the Westport School. Fifth grade." The commercials were on now but Tucker continued to keep his eyes on the screen. "How come you wanted to see me?" he asked again.

Maggie swallowed. This Tucker was not what she'd expected. That, and his being so young, made things different.

Tucker rolled over and stared at her from the floor. "How come?"

Maggie said, "Were you trying to . . . shoot the heron?"

Tucker studied her with eyes that Maggie could not read. Then he rolled back around to stare at the screen. "Sure," he finally said. "What's it to you?"

CHAPTER

19

As Maggie looked at Tucker, who continued to watch the television cartoons placidly, all she could think was, this is *not* the way things are supposed to happen. She had read mysteries. Watched them. Usually they were fun. And they all seemed to work the same way: A detective struggled long and hard to find the criminal. When the criminal was found, he confessed. Then the story came to a neat end.

But, here she was, having gathered and followed the clues of the crime. It had allowed her to discover the criminal quickly. What's more, the criminal *had* just confessed. It was something of a shock then to suddenly realize that those mystery stories never did reveal what happened next. This certainly was not the end.

Tucker was lying on the floor watching TV, and he did not even seem to care that he *had* confessed. What was she to do?

"But . . . why?" Maggie finally asked him.

"Why *what*?"

Maggie looked at him incredulously. "You know. . . . *Why* did you shoot at the heron?"

The action on the screen exploded with mayhem. In spite of herself, Maggie looked around. A brawl between superheroes was taking place. She watched. It was only when the commercial came on that she remembered she had asked Tucker a question and that he had not bothered to answer.

Apparently, he did not remember her question. He got up and all he said was, "Want some popcorn?"

Maggie shook her head. "No," she said.

Tucker went out of the room. From somewhere in the house—the kitchen, Maggie guessed—she heard him move about.

The program on the TV resumed. It was not long before Tucker returned with a large bowl of popcorn.

"Microwave makes it fast," he explained. "Sure you don't want some?"

"Not hungry."

"I know a kid with braces," Tucker said. "He's not allowed to have any at all." He sat down cross-legged on the carpet. Almost immediately his attention went back to the screen.

After a moment Maggie said, "Aren't you going to tell me *why* you shot at the heron?"

"What?"

"The *heron*," Maggie said, hearing the exasperation in her voice and not liking it.

"Oh, that," Tucker said. He shrugged. "I felt like it."

"That's no reason."

"Sure it is."

"But . . . it's . . . beautiful," Maggie cried.

"It's just a bird. . . " Tucker said indifferently.

Maggie stared at him. Suddenly angry, she got up and stood between him and the TV screen. "Will you talk to me!" she said.

"Hey, out of the way!" Tucker called. "I'm trying to watch!"

"You shouldn't do it," Maggie said.

"Do what? What are you *talking* about? Would you get out of the way!" Suddenly he squirmed forward and batted her legs, forcing her to move.

"You were trying to kill the heron," she said. "That's wrong!"

This time Tucker turned from the TV to look up at her. To her surprise she saw real puzzlement on his face.

"I don't want you to shoot at the heron!"

"What are you, some kind of bird cop or something?"

Maggie, feeling increasingly frustrated, stamped her foot. "You have no right to kill the bird!"

Tucker turned his attention back to the screen. "I can

kill anything I want to," he informed her. "In case you hadn't noticed, it's a free country." Maggie, not knowing what to do, sat down on an easy chair. Tucker, after momentarily looking at her, went back to the television.

When a few minutes had passed Maggie said, "I mean, it *is* probably against the law. Besides, you shouldn't kill beautiful things."

"You really are a nut."

"I *mean* it."

"So what? I mean it, too."

Maggie, completely stymied, looked at Tucker uncomprehendingly. All of a sudden the absurdity of the situation came over her. Before she could suppress it, she laughed.

Tucker looked around. "What's so funny?" he demanded.

"Do you have any idea what I'm talking about?"

Tucker studied her. For the first time since he had answered the door, Maggie had the sensation that he was really looking at her, paying attention. But as to what he was thinking behind that bland face, she had not the slightest idea.

"Do you?" she repeated.

"Do I *what*?"

"Have any idea what I'm talking about?"

"You're some nut," he said with authority. "People who could eat popcorn but won't are nuts."

"The bird, stupid!" she yelled at him.

At her outburst, his eyes widened. Then he laughed. "I like you," he said. "I really do. You're a nut."

Not knowing what to say or do, Maggie got up. She looked at Tucker, whose attention was once again glued to the television.

"Can I see your house?"

"Sure," Tucker said, making no move. After a moment Maggie began to wander through the house.

It was all on one level and in fact much smaller inside than it had appeared from the outside. There was a large bedroom, painted white, which, she assumed, belonged to Tucker's parents. It was very neat and, other than a couple of pieces of furniture, almost completely empty.

Tucker's room—she guessed it was his—was completely tidy, too. That surprised her. The bed was made. A few toys were neatly stacked in a bookcase. On the pale blue wall were two posters, one of a baseball player, the other a football player.

There were two bathrooms, one large one and one small, both tiled.

And there was another bedroom. Maggie decided it must be a girl's room because the bed was covered with a pink coverlet. A teddy bear was propped against a red pillow. There was also a small dressing table set before a mirror, the table edged with lacy frill. Perfume and lipstick stood side by side. Two pictures of rock stars were on the wall. Maggie did not recognize who they were.

Maggie went into the kitchen. It was painted in bright yellows and whites and also had lots of tiles. It, too, was sparkling clean.

Her survey complete, Maggie returned to the living room. Tucker was still on his stomach, watching TV. It was if he had not moved. She studied him for a while.

"That all you do, watch TV?" she asked.

"What's it to you?" he returned.

"It's summer," she said, trying to be sarcastic.

"Well, sometimes I get out in my father's dumb raft and go out into the dumb marsh to this dumb island and watch this dumb girl watch this dumb bird in this dumb place."

Maggie, shocked, stared at him. "You mean you've been watching me?"

"Sure. My parents go off to work early. I do what I want. When I'm older I'm going to be a spy."

Maggie found her head in a whirl. This boy was really crazy. "What do they do?" she asked, not knowing what else to say.

"My father has a tile store in New Bedford. My mother is a dental hygienist." He grinned broadly. "No cavities."

"Do you have any brothers?"

Tucker shook his head.

"What about a sister?"

"She got killed."

"*Killed?*"

"Auto accident. Some dumb drunk driver. She was

twelve. I was only two." He lifted an arm. "I have a scar on the back of my neck. You can see it in decent light. Want to? I was almost killed." He spoke with pride.

Maggie shook her head.

"She's buried over at St. Francis Cemetery. That's in Tiverton."

"I'm sorry."

Tucker shrugged.

After a moment Maggie said, "What do you do all day?"

"Nothing."

"Don't you have friends?"

"Sure. Lots."

"Well?"

"They live a few miles away."

"I saw a bike," Maggie said.

"It's too far."

With a rising feeling of despair, Maggie went to the door. She opened it.

"Sure you don't want some popcorn?" Tucker said without looking around.

She shook her head. "Tucker . . ."

"What . . . ?"

"Don't kill the heron. . . ."

"Why?"

"I love it."

That time he turned around to look at her. "You really are a nut," he said, and swiveled back around onto his belly, cupped his chin in his hands, and set his eyes on the TV screen once again. "You really are."

Maggie studied Tucker for a moment, then went out the door, letting it slam behind her as an expression of anger. The sunlight, hot and bright, a contrast to the dimness inside the house, blinded her momentarily. Feeling a little dizzy, she sat down on the deck steps and tried to grasp what had just happened.

She had done exactly what she had set out to do. She had found the one who was trying to harm the heron. Yet now it all seemed more hopeless than before.

Heavyhearted, Maggie allowed herself the pleasure of thinking of Tucker as crazy. Really crazy. Even as she thought it, she knew that was too easy. He was not crazy. He just did not care.

How do you deal with someone who just does not care what they do?

She tried to think of stories she had read in which that had happened. But all the villains she had ever read about always cared a lot. They were really selfish, or terribly greedy, madly jealous. . . . She could make a list of all the strong emotions. But as for a character who just didn't care . . . she could not think of one. It really disturbed her.

She looked back and studied the house. It made her think of one of the shells she and her father had found on the beach, but she knew Tucker was inside watching TV.

 *When Maggie returned* to the cottage, she found that Joanna had spread a blanket on the grass and was now lying on her back, holding Linda up in the air. Every now and then she gave the baby a shake. Each time, Linda broke into a wide grin and gurgled with pleasure.

Maggie flopped down on the grass nearby.

"Out on the lake?" Joanna asked.

"By the marsh."

"You do like it there," Joanna said, "don't you?"

"It's pretty."

Joanna shook the baby. Linda gurgled. "I love it when she smiles like that," Joanna said. She sat up and put the baby down by her side. "Your dad said something about the two of you going to the movies Monday night."

Maggie squinted up at Joanna. "Is that all right?"

"Oh, sure. I made a deal with him. I said yes if he'd let you and me go to church in the morning, just us. Would you like to?"

"What about Linda?"

"I can take her."

"Okay."

After a pensive moment Joanna said, "When you go out, do you think you could talk to him about the medicine?"

"I'll try."

"Good girl."

Maggie looked around. "Where is he?"

"Inside. On the phone. Maggie, I'm feeling bad about dumping this on you. Not much of a vacation, is it?"

Maggie caught the echo of her father's same question. "It's fine," she said.

Joanna reached out and patted Maggie's hand. "You're a great kid. You really are."

Maggie flushed with pleasure. "Thanks."

Then after a moment, Joanna said, "You're worried. Is it what I was telling you about? About your father and me?"

Maggie shook her head.

"Something else?"

Maggie nodded.

"Want to tell me what it is?"

For a moment Maggie considered telling Joanna all about the heron and Tucker. Just as quickly she decided it was her own business. And impossible to explain.

Not knowing what to say, she only shook her head, then turned to watch Linda. The baby was staring with great intensity at one of her own feet. Maggie could almost watch her mind struggling to comprehend what she was seeing. "Joanna," she said.

"Hmmmm."

"How do people get to be the way they are?"

The magnitude of the question made Joanna laugh. "Why, what do you mean?"

"People are so complicated!" Maggie burst out.

"Told you!"

"But how can you figure out why people *do* things?"

"Wait. Watch."

"For what?"

"Until you understand."

"But what if you *still* can't understand?"

"I suppose if you care enough you keep doing the same, waiting and watching."

"But, I mean, do you ever get to know?" Maggie wondered. "Really know?"

Joanna smiled. Maggie saw her eyes shift toward the house. "I used to think so." She looked down at Linda and patted the baby's belly. "Look at her. Four months old. She hasn't exactly lived what you'd call a long life. But I'm already trying to keep up with her."

"Don't you know her?" Maggie asked, surprised.

"Before she was born I thought I would. I said to myself, 'Joanna, this baby is going to be the one person you really know.' "

"Don't you?"

"A lot," Joanna said with a shy smile. "But not all. Not by a long shot."

"Will you ever?"

Joanna laughed. "I'm beginning to doubt it."

"Does that make you feel bad?"

"I don't think so."

"How come?"

"Well, maybe she's telling me it's time I studied myself."

Maggie sat on her rock. Twenty feet beyond, wading in the marsh waters, was the heron. It had not been there at first. It was only after a long wait, when Maggie was about to leave, that the bird had arrived. Now she studied it thoughtfully. As always, she thought of how beautiful it was. How graceful. How oblivious it seemed to be of her and the rest of the world.

And yet Maggie knew with a certainty that it *was* aware of her. That it was *not* oblivious. Though it did not appear to fear her, it was aware of her in the same way the bird seemed to know that there was danger on the little island even as it moved slowly toward it.

Maggie studied the island. Perhaps Tucker was there

right now. Watching the heron. Watching her. Waiting to kill the heron.

For what felt like the millionth time, Maggie asked herself why Tucker would want to kill such a beautiful thing. No matter how hard she thought, she could find no reason.

CHAPTER
21

In Seattle, Maggie and her mother did not go to church very often. When they did go, it was to the nearby St. Martin's Episcopalian Church on Christmas Eve. A few times they had attended a Catholic church (Maggie did not even know its name) for Easter services. As for her father's religion, Maggie was not certain about that, or even if he had any. At least she never knew him to attend any kind of religious service.

So it was that during Sunday breakfast, when Joanna reminded her that they were going to church, Maggie asked, "Do I have to *do* anything?"

"Nothing. No real dressing up either. Just look decent."

Maggie automatically looked toward her father. "I

have some calls to make," he said in response to her unasked question.

Joanna touched Maggie's arm. "Just us," Joanna reminded her.

"And the baby," Mr. Lavchek interjected.

Forty-five minutes later, Joanna, Maggie, and the baby were on their way. "You know," Joanna said, "though I was brought up to be religious, I'm not. As a kid I was always told to go to army base services. And I did. Wasn't as if my parents went. Maybe that's why I disliked it. But lately . . . well, it can be very soothing. I need a bit of that."

"Is Congre—" Maggie forgot the word.

"Congregational."

"Is Congregational your church?" Maggie asked.

Joanna shook her head. "I was brought up Methodist. But I like this church building. Classic New England. Has a nice quiet feeling to it. I think you'll like it, too."

Joanna was right. Maggie did like the building. It was all wood and old, painted a creamy white with a tall steeple. As they pulled into the parking lot, there came the sound of a bell tolling.

"Is there a bell up there?" Maggie asked. She could not see one.

Joanna giggled. "I think it's a recording. But it's nice anyway."

The interior was also white but trimmed with brightly polished wood. A sweet, almost crisp smell perfumed the air. Maggie was reminded of her mother's cedar closet. There was very little inside besides pews. And not many people were in attendance, either, no more than thirty, which included a scattering of kids.

Joanna, almost as much a stranger as Maggie was, introduced herself as a summer renter to the usher who greeted them. She presented Maggie as "my Seattle, Washington, daughter."

The usher, an old, bald man, formally shook hands first with Joanna then Maggie and said he was "charmed" to meet them both. But he was most interested in Linda and made a toothless grin at her. Linda stared at him, opening her own toothless mouth.

"I'll sit toward the back," Joanna told the usher. "At the side. In case the baby makes a fuss."

"That's perfectly fine," the usher said with another smile.

When they took their places Maggie noticed an old wall clock, which ticked pleasantly. At ten o'clock it whirred and chimed the hours with soft pinging sounds. People stopped their neighborly chatting and became quiet. Some bowed their heads. Others stared straight ahead. A few seemed to have their eyes focused some-where up above.

A young minister, his face tan, his robe black, came forward. The service began. Maggie watched it all. At first she was interested but soon became bored. Fortu-nately, their pew, off to the side, allowed her to see people's faces. She found herself studying them, wondering what they were thinking, feeling. One person had a fixed smile. Another a frown. Most faces, however, appeared perfectly placid and gave no clue at all to what thoughts they contained.

Linda gave a bit of a cry. By the time Maggie turned, Joanna was nursing her. No one seemed to have noticed.

Maggie searched about for the kids. Her eyes fastened on one boy who looked vaguely familiar. He was sitting very still. With a bit of a shock, Maggie realized it was Tucker, but with his hair so slicked down—which made his ears stick out—and dressed so neatly in a light blue summer suit and tie that he seemed a different person. As for his face, seen in profile, it was just as bland as she recalled, almost masklike, she decided. After watching for a while she realized she could not guess his thoughts here any more than she could in his house. She found herself wondering if he even had thoughts.

He was seated next to two grown-ups, a man and a woman—Tucker was next to the woman—who Maggie guessed were his parents. They, too, were in neatly pressed summer suits.

Maggie tried to match the image of Tucker in his home—watching cartoons, being rude to her—with this Tucker, so quiet and respectful. She could not.

There was some singing, which Maggie liked. Then the minister talked and Maggie tried to follow what he was saying. It was something about the gifts of summer, mixed in with the blessings of the Almighty and the hard labor of ordinary folk. He mentioned the homeless. The unemployed. God's responsibility and people's responsibilities. Maggie had the feeling he was asking people to do something, but exactly what, she could not be sure.

Joanna had stopped nursing. The baby was asleep. But it was Joanna who had a dreamy look on her face. Once again Maggie thought how pretty she was. Now, however, she could see sadness, too. Maggie wondered if it had been there before and if she was only noticing now.

Maggie looked around. To her surprise Tucker had twisted about and was looking right at her. Without changing the somber expression on his face, he winked.

Caught by surprise, Maggie almost laughed but caught herself. Instead, she bit down on her lip and looked away.

She tried not to look at Tucker again but gave in. He was still staring at her. The moment she faced him he did as he had done before—winked.

Maggie shifted her body about so it was harder to see him. He was trying to make her laugh and it irritated her. It took her a moment to figure out that Tucker was acting as if they were friends. She did not want to be his friend. In fact, she hated him.

Hate him? Why did she dislike him so much? It bothered her. But the next moment she told herself that it was perfectly reasonable *and* right to hate him. After all, he wanted to kill the heron. He had said so himself. But here he was, dressed up, listening to all this talk about goodness, doing silly stuff as if they were friends.

It took an effort to keep from looking around at him but Maggie managed it for a long time. But then, unable to resist, she turned again. As before she found his eyes on her. Once more he winked. That time she was sure his mouth was trying to keep from smiling.

She grimaced at him and looked away and attempted to pay attention to the minister. She could no longer follow what he was saying. In spite of herself, she found herself stealing glances at Tucker.

He was still staring at her. This time Maggie decided to glare back, as if to challenge him. Even as she watched, she saw the man she'd decided was Tucker's father slowly lift his arm, put it behind his wife, then begin to slide it along the pew toward Tucker. It moved like a snake. Suddenly, Maggie realized what the man was about to do. Horrified, she wanted to call out, to warn Tucker, but caught herself just in time. In any case, at that very moment, Tucker's father, with a sharp, whiplike snap of his hand, struck the side of Tucker's face. The sound—a crack—cut through the minister's words like a sharp gunshot—there one moment, gone the next.

Tucker, taken completely by surprise, started to spin around, only to freeze. Slowly he turned to face front.

As Maggie watched, the father's hand withdrew.

Tucker, his face beet-red, sat without moving, his eyes fixed on the minister. For the rest of the service— Maggie watched—he did not move. Not an inch.

The service ended. People stood up and began to file out. Maggie searched for Tucker. He was in the aisle, his father leaning over at him, talking. Tucker was staring down at his feet.

"Let's go," Joanna said.

The young minister was standing at the door greeting and chatting with people as they left.

While Joanna talked to him briefly, Maggie looked again for Tucker. She did not see him until they were driving out of the lot. He was in a car whose windows were closed. He was alone, sitting rigidly in the backseat, staring straight forward.

CHAPTER
22

"*I thought we were going* after dinner," Maggie said as her father drove the car along the narrow, rutted road that led from the cabin. It was Monday and though the sun was still shining, the road seemed caught in a net of shadows.

"This is serious stuff," her father replied. "We'll eat out, go to a movie, grab some ice cream. Make a night of it. Like it?"

"Sure."

"All right then."

After a moment Maggie said, "I just sort of feel bad about leaving Joanna and Linda."

"Rather be with her than me?" her father snapped.

Maggie, taken aback, said, "No."

"She's got her baby."

Maggie stole a glance at her father. He looked grim. "Was that an important call you got?" she asked.

Mr. Lavchek had been on the phone for half an hour before they left. Right after hanging up, he insisted they leave.

"All calls are important."

They pulled out of the woods and headed down a regular road.

"Look," Mr. Lavchek said, breaking the silence since his last remark, "I'm sure it's not exactly a secret. Joanna and I are not hitting it off so well lately."

Maggie kept her eyes in front of her.

"Or maybe you didn't notice."

Maggie shook her head.

"Does that expressive body language mean you did or did not notice?" her father demanded.

"I noticed."

"Okay then. Look, it's no big deal. Happens to lots of perfectly well-married people."

Maggie, her eyes glued to the road before them, began to wish her father would turn around and go back to the cabin. As it was, the next moment Mr. Lavchek veered sharply off to the side of the road and stopped the car.

"What's the matter?" Maggie said, alarmed.

"Look, kid," he said grimly, "either the two of us are going to have a nice time together or we're not going to do this. I don't need a night of sulks. I thought this would be fun. This is the first time we've been out alone, you know. Now, what's it going to be? Yes or no?"

"Yes or no what?"

"Are we going out?"

"If you want to."

"Do you want to?"

"Yes."

"All right then. But that includes talk. You as well as me. That clear?"

After she gave a curt nod, Mr. Lavchek started the car up again.

Maggie, thinking but not saying that her father was a bully, clenched her fists tightly. She wondered what he would do if she started to cry—she felt like it, but was determined not to. Even so, for a while there was nothing but strained silence between them.

Then her father—his voice more relaxed—said, "We've got some choices for dinner. I suppose we can go to some fast-food place. But there is a decent seafood restaurant out by Goose Neck Beach. No big deal. But nice."

"Seafood place," she said.

"Great." He looked at his watch. "Actually, let's do the movie first. Makes things less pressured. We'll get some popcorn to tide you over. Okay?"

"Fine," Maggie said, hoping her father would not notice she was just agreeing to everything he said. As they drove, Maggie wondered how she was ever going to speak to him about the medicine. She knew he would be furious. Still, if there was one thing that justified leaving Joanna behind it was her promise. Maggie was determined to try.

They reached the multimovie theater in plenty of time to stand in line for popcorn.

"Did you know movie theaters often make more money selling popcorn than they do from ticket sales?"

Maggie shook her head. She had not known.

"True. What do you like? Salt? Butter? The works?"

"Whatever."

"They speak English in Seattle?" Mr. Lavchek asked while purchasing the biggest bucket available.

Maggie refused to respond.

They were walking toward their theater when Maggie felt a sharp tug on her arm. She stopped and turned. It was Tucker. He was grinning broadly.

"Hey, Big Bird," he said. "Thought you didn't like popcorn."

Maggie, taken completely by surprise, could only murmur, "Oh, hi." There was a woman right behind Tucker whom Maggie recognized as his mother.

"What are you seeing?" Tucker asked Maggie.

"*Magic Crystal*," she answered lamely.

"Wouldn't catch me dead watching that dumb stuff. I'm seeing *Attack Zero*."

"Let's go, Tucker," the woman said impatiently. She

nodded and smiled to Maggie. Maggie thought the smile phony.

"See you later, Big Bird," Tucker called, and he and his mother disappeared into the crowd.

"Who was that?" Mr. Lavchek asked, gazing after them.

"Kid named Tucker. He lives on the other side of the marsh."

"When did you meet him?"

"Before."

"Miss Secret-Social-Life," her father teased. "How come he called you Big Bird?"

"I don't know," Maggie lied.

"Isn't he a little young for you?"

"Dad . . . !"

"Sorry! Forget I said anything. Come on. We need to find decent seats."

Maggie could not keep her mind on the movie. She kept thinking about Tucker and how he had greeted her, as if she were his friend. It made her think about what had happened at church. Like then, he actually smiled, something she could not remember him doing when she was at his house.

Maggie decided—though she knew she was being unfair—that she did not like his mother. She was not sure why. Perhaps it was that fake smile. Whatever she thought about Tucker, at least when he smiled it was not fake.

But it was Tucker's calling her "Big Bird" that kept going through Maggie's mind. Despite what she had said to her father, she knew exactly why he had called her that. The heron. He was teasing her, yes, but why tease her about *that*?

The more she thought about it, the more she sensed the teasing had to mean something else than just the bird. Perhaps in some way—a way she had not noticed—she *had* made an impression on him. The question was—and it was one she kept asking herself—what *kind* of impression?

Feeling guilty that she was paying little attention to the movie, Maggie glanced around at her father. He had fallen asleep.

"Not bad. Not bad," Mr. Lavchek said as they filed out when the film was over.

Maggie, knowing he had missed most of it, only said, "It was fun." She was doing one of her favorite things: watching the faces of those lined up to go into the movie. Some time ago she had decided that that situation was one of the few times when people *wanted* you to look at them; it was because they were trying to figure out what the audience *leaving* the theater thought of the movie. So if the movie had been sad, she would smile broadly. If it had been funny, she would try to look tragic.

"Do you still like fantasy and magic as much as you used to?" her father asked.

"I suppose," she replied.

"You're old enough to know it's just escapism."

"What's that mean?"

"It's kind of cheap, easy, and mostly on-the-sly religion."

"I like magic."

"Okay. Why?"

Maggie had an image of herself flying into Providence wishing her father was the same as he had been. It had not worked, of course. Suddenly she knew she had misunderstood the purpose of magic.

"Come on. Why do you like magic?" her father repeated.

"You always told me to," she replied, stalling so as to think out her new thoughts.

"That was then. You're older. What's in it for you now?"

"I used to think magic could keep things—you know—so they wouldn't change."

"And now?"

Maggie, trying to catch up with her own ideas, considered for a moment. Then she said, "I guess it has nothing to do with changing. See, the marsh isn't magic. But—if you *think* of it as magic, you see it . . . differently." Even as she spoke, Maggie could see the heron. "Right. It's a different way of seeing."

"Seeing what?"

"What else is there."

Mr. Lavchek thought a moment. Then, as though dismissing the idea, he said, "Come on. Let's go eat."

CHAPTER

23

Each table at the Goose Neck Café had a
red-and-white checked tablecloth as well
as a candle stuck in a wine bottle.

"I'm starved," Mr. Lavchek said, handing
Maggie a menu.

"Me, too." She studied the list of possibilities, then
put down the folder. "You order for me. I don't know
what this stuff is."

"Fine." He beckoned the waitress over and told her
what they wanted.

"Anything to drink?" the waitress asked.

"Ginger ale," Maggie said.

Mr. Lavchek ordered some beer.

"You shouldn't drink beer and drive, too," Maggie
told him.

Her father wagged his head. "The best part of having a child is that they tell you what's best for you."

Maggie, stung, blurted out, "Well, you *should* take your medicine." The words, spoken without premeditation, surprised her as much as her father. She stared at her father, frightened by what she had done. His face, which had been soft and friendly a moment before, had stiffened.

"What's that supposed to mean?" he demanded.

Trapped, but knowing no way to stop what she had begun, Maggie whispered, "You don't take your medicine."

"What medicine?"

"For your heart. It's in the bathroom cabinet. You . . . never opened the bottles."

"Is this something Joanna told you?" He was very angry.

Maggie shook her head.

"Talk!" Mr. Lavchek barked.

People at a nearby table turned their heads.

"Dad . . ." Maggie cautioned.

"I want an answer!"

"I found out myself," Maggie said. She was trembling, trying to keep her voice low. "And I told her. You aren't taking the medicine that you're supposed to take."

"That's only an extra supply," he returned.

"Dad . . ." Maggie pleaded.

"Are you saying I'm lying to you?"

"Dad . . ."

"Are you?" His face had turned red with anger. "Answer me!"

More people turned about. Maggie, horrified, felt like crawling under the table.

The waitress approached them. "Is something the matter?" she asked.

"Mind your own business!" Mr. Lavchek snapped. He was staring at Maggie. But the waitress stayed close, reluctant to leave.

The next second Maggie's father leaped up, knocking his chair back onto the floor with a crash. The waitress jumped. Wheeling about, Mr. Lavchek marched out of the restaurant.

For a moment Maggie remained sitting, not believing what was happening. Then, heart pounding, trying to hold on to her dignity, she managed to get up. Feeling nothing but humiliation beneath the stares of everyone in the restaurant, she followed her father.

Once outside she stood before the restaurant door and searched for her father. When she could not find him, she was sure she was going to die.

From across the parking lot she heard the noise of a motor starting up. She raced toward it. Headlights burst on.

"Dad!" she cried, threading her way frantically through the cars. "Dad!"

Breathless, she reached the car, pulled open the door,

and leaped in. Mr. Lavchek, without even looking at her, flung the car forward. With wheels spinning the gravel, the car shot out of the parking lot.

They were roaring down the road much too fast. Maggie could not keep the tears from coming. "Dad," she said. "I'm sorry. I didn't mean to make you so angry. I'm sorry. Please stop the car. Please!"

Mr. Lavchek, gripping the wheel with two tight fists, his jaw jutting forward, kept his eyes straight forward.

"Would you let me explain," Maggie cried. "Will you let me!"

The car picked up speed as it tore down a straight stretch. Maggie's heart hammered.

"You're going too fast. Please stop! Dad, I just don't want anything to happen to you. That's why I said that about the medicine. Please stop!"

Behind them, at a distance, a siren began to wail. Mr. Lavchek glanced up at his rearview mirror and swore. Maggie had never heard him swear like that before. She glanced back. A frenzy of flickering lights were right behind them and drawing closer. The siren screamed.

For just a moment their own car picked up speed.

"Dad, you have to stop!" Maggie pleaded.

Mr. Lavchek braked sharply, swerved off to the side of the road, and came to a lurching halt. The siren and lights seemed to explode behind them.

With frightened eyes Maggie watched as her father bent over and pressed his forehead to the wheel.

"Good evening, sir," came a brisk voice. "May I see your license, registration, and insurance papers, please."

Maggie, breathing a sigh of relief, sank back in her seat.

"How much is it?" Maggie asked.

Her father was staring bleakly at the ticket the policeman had given him. "One hundred and twenty-five dollars."

"That's so much!"

"I was going fast." He folded the ticket with elaborate care and placed it in a shirt pocket. Then he leaned his head back against the seat and rubbed his eyes.

"Are you okay?" Maggie asked.

"Yes," he said, but kept his hands over his eyes. It was as if the night were not dark enough for him. Then, after a while, he said, "No, I'm not."

Maggie waited for him to say more, but when he didn't, she whispered, "What's the matter?"

"A lot of things."

Maggie watched him, torn between wanting him to explain and wishing he would not. In the end Mr. Lavchek only gave a little shake of his head, as if he had been arguing with himself. He started up the motor and put it in gear. The car lurched back onto the road. Rather slowly now, driving in silence, they headed for home.

Maggie, much relieved, kept her eyes on the insects that were like tiny diamonds swirling in the twin tunnels of the headlight beams. Now and again—as she waited for her father to speak—she glanced over at him. In the dim panel light his face was the color of old and brittle yellow paper.

They reached the dirt road. When they entered it Mr. Lavchek slowed even more. The car's headlights lit up rows of slender tree trunks. It was as if they had entered a gigantic cage.

Without warning Maggie's father stopped the car and turned off all the lights. The darkness was intense, filled with nothing but the ceaseless chatter of crickets. Maggie sat up straighter to see if she could see the log cabin. She could not.

Tensely, she waited for her father to speak. It took a long while. First he sighed. Then he said, "I'm sorry . . . I lost my temper." He sounded enormously tired.

"That's okay."

"No. No. It's not okay. The fact is . . ." Mr. Lavchek did not finish his sentence.

Maggie squeezed her hands until they hurt, but it was

better than the pain gathering in her chest. She was certain her father was about to say things she did not want to hear.

"I'm not . . ." Mr. Lavchek managed to say, "I'm not even sure I know why I got so angry. You were only telling me something I knew. You're right. Of course, you're right. I haven't been taking the medicine. I . . . I never even started."

When he did not continue, Maggie said, "How come?"

"Maggie, you can ask—and believe me I ask myself that any number of times every day—but I'm not sure I have an answer."

"But if the doctor—" Maggie tried to say.

Her father interrupted. "Look," he said, "if I take the medicine, that means I'm sick. If I'm sick that means something's the matter with me. And if something is the . . ." He paused before going on, as if he were walking up a steep hill and needed to gather strength for each step. "And if there is something the matter with me . . . my heart, I—" Once again he stopped.

Maggie tried to look at him but in the darkness she could only make out the dimmest of outlines.

"It's all nonsense," he said suddenly, as if bursting onto the summit of his frustration.

"What is?"

Mr. Lavchek sniffed a few times. When Maggie looked at him she could tell his head was bent forward and he was pressing his hands to his face.

"Maggie," he finally said, "I'm . . . I'm very . . . frightened." Each word seemed an effort and sounded as though it came from a great distance.

Maggie, shocked by his words, his manner, all the same reached out and touched his arm. After a moment he grasped the hand with both of his. To her surprise he drew the hand to his lips and kissed her fingers.

"Why?" she found the strength to ask. "Why are you frightened?"

"Because . . . Maggie, I might die," he said at last. "And I don't want to." He retreated back into silence. Then again he sighed, and this time said, "Maggie, this marriage with Joanna . . . it was a mistake . . . and the baby . . . a mistake, too . . . and what I do . . . my work . . . all a waste of time. A bloody waste. It doesn't matter. It never has. It never will. None of it. Absolutely none. In high school we used to say, 'Nothing matters very much, and what matters matters very little.' Oh, that's so true. So very true."

It was the sound of his words even more than their meaning that appalled Maggie. It was as if he were wrapped—mummylike—in pain and was speaking through layers upon layers of it.

"Why do you think that?" she whispered.

"Because I keep making mistakes. Keep botching things."

"What?"

"I just told you. . . . Nothing I do . . . matters.

Maggie tried desperately to think of what to say. "Dad?"

"What?"

"Did . . . the doctor say you'd . . . die?"

Mr. Lavchek lifted his head. "He said that if I didn't take care of myself I'd get a heart attack. A stroke. Die."

Maggie thought for a moment. Then carefully, she said, "Then he didn't say you *would* die?"

"It amounts to the same thing."

"It doesn't!" she protested with a forcefulness that surprised herself.

"Don't be childish!" he snapped.

Maggie flung herself back in her seat. "You are *so* stupid!" she cried in desperation.

"Don't talk to me like that!" he exploded with venom. "That's all I get. Criticism! What the crap do you know? People take care of you. You do what you want. Nothing to worry about. You get up each morning and trot on down to that dead bog and stare at some bird. Don't be surprised I know! I'm surrounded by people—kids— who think they know something but just haven't the brains to know how profoundly ignorant they are. Joanna!" he sneered. "Mention World War II, and she thinks I'm talking about a movie sequel."

"She loves you!"

"Oh, stop it! What the hell do you know about love!"

"She does! And if you'd be with her, Linda would love you, too."

"Muck! Absolute muck! What do you think all these calls are about! I am trying to find a job because three months ago I was fired! After twenty-seven years—fired! Laid off! Dropped! Booted! Ousted! Ejected! Dumped! Ditched! Let go! Dismissed! Retired! Deposed! Terminated! Kicked out! Bunch of kids—kids half my age, none of my experience—buy the company and"—Mr. Lavchek snapped his fingers—"I'm out. Like that. Like that! They don't know me. They don't *want* to know me. Just like that. Out. I saw it coming. Saw it happen to others. But I didn't believe it. Didn't want to believe it. Oh, no, not me, I said. That's not going to happen to me. It can't happen to me. I've done everything right. Knew the rules. Wrote the rules! Did what I was supposed to do. Played the game. I'm told I'm good. I was good. *Am* good. But it's worthless. Worthless! I'm out. Out! Out! Out! And no matter how much I try, ask, beg, plead, grovel, I can't get another job. The only way I'm worth anything is if I die."

"That's not so!"

"It is so!" Mr. Lavchek roared, in a complete rage now, squirming frantically on the seat as though trying to get off a leash, beating his fists against the steering wheel.

"Dad, I love you!"

He spun around to face her. Though it was dark she could see how contorted his features were. "Oh, sure, you *love* me," he said sarcastically. "And when the judge asked you who you wanted to live with, you didn't miss a beat. Not a one! Your mother, you said. Don't tell me you love me! What do you think these visits are? You're a hostage. If you don't come, I don't pay your mother to keep you! Get out of the car," he screamed at her. "The cabin is right over there. For once I'd like some time for myself!"

Maggie, frozen with horror, could not budge.

"Didn't you hear me? Out!" He lunged across her and flung open the door. "Get out!"

Maggie swiveled around and somehow managed to step out of the car. Mr. Lavchek reached over and yanked the door shut. Then he started up the motor, flicked on the headlights, and began to back down the road very fast.

"Dad!" Maggie cried to him. "Dad!" Tears were streaming down her cheeks. But as she watched, the headlights kept retreating through the woods like a movie running backward. Then the car swung about, the white beams slicing scythelike through the trees. Within moments, she could hear wheels spinning on dirt, and finally, the sound of the car roaring away.

Maggie remained where she was, trying to press down her grief. But the tears were coming too fast and she soon gave up the effort. Then, knowing she could not just stand there, she turned down the road and began to walk slowly in the direction of the cabin.

"He's such a bully," she kept repeating to herself. That, she knew, was the least of it. Her father's life was in a state of disaster. She thought how unfair it all was for her. None of this was her problem. The next moment she scolded herself for being uncaring, selfish, and mean. He was upset. He did not know what he was saying. He needed help. Her help. But what was *she* to do?

Within moments she saw the cabin windows shining golden through the trees. She stopped. Briefly, she had a vision of herself—as though in a fairy tale—coming upon a good magician's hut in a forest. The magician would make it all right. Ruefully, she reminded herself that that was the old magic. And anyway, this was *not* going to be a magical moment of any kind.

To begin with, what was she going to say to Joanna? It was sinking in that Joanna probably did not know much of what Maggie now knew. She, Maggie, would have to tell her. And it was all so horrible. Wistfully, she glanced in the direction of the marsh, as if an escape lay that way. But there wasn't any, and she knew it. She had to go to Joanna. Making a vague attempt to wipe away her tears she went forward.

"Hi!"

As Maggie came through the door Joanna greeted her gaily. She was seated on the couch, reading, a shawl over her shoulders. Linda was in her cradle, asleep. But Maggie had hardly taken another step when Joanna realized something was wrong.

"What's the matter?" she asked, thrusting aside her book. "Where's Alan?"

Maggie stood for a moment trying to find her voice.

"Maggie, where is he?"

"It was about the medicine," Maggie blurted out. "I told him, you know, that he wasn't taking any, and he blew up. Really blew up. I've never seen him like that. He was saying all these . . . crazy things. . . . And then . . . he made me get out of the car and drove off. Just now."

"Oh my God . . ." Joanna said. She leaped off the couch and hurried to Maggie, taking her in her arms. "How awful!"

Maggie, sniffling, nodded.

"But, did you see a movie and eat . . . ?"

Maggie nodded to the first, shook her head to the second.

Joanna grasped Maggie's hands. "You're cold and hungry. I'll make you an omelet. Put this shawl around you. Let's get some tea first." She fluttered about, banging the kettle onto the stove, pulling out a frying pan, opening the fridge.

Maggie collapsed onto a stool, her feet hooked on the highest rung, and gazed mournfully at the floor. She was trying to understand what had happened, trying to think what—and how—she was going to tell everything—the worst parts—to Joanna. Thankfully, Joanna was too involved in the cooking to ask questions.

Suddenly, into Maggie's mind came one of the things her father had said, that he had known she had been watching the bird. *How* did he know? Why hadn't he said anything before? Why did it make him so angry?

"Good. Here's your tea," Joanna called to her.

Maggie approached and Joanna thrust a hot mug at her. Milk had been mixed in—not the way Maggie liked it—but she was not about to object. Instead, feeling only grateful that Joanna was there, she sank back on the stool and sipped slowly.

"I'll have this done in a moment. Toast? Jam? Bacon?"

"No bacon. But the rest. . . . Thank you."

"Coming right up. Now, if you can, tell me what happened."

"Joanna . . ."

"What?"

"It's bad."

Joanna stared at her. "Tell me."

It took a while and Maggie was finished eating by the time she was done, but bit by bit she related a good deal—not all—of what her father had told her.

Joanna had listened, now and then shaking her head, looking more and more stricken. When Maggie related her father's news that he had been fired, she gasped.

"When did it happen?" she asked.

"He said three months ago."

"Three . . . ! My God. . . ."

"He didn't tell, did he?"

Joanna began to pace about in an agitated manner. "Did he?"

Joanna shook her head. "Not a word. I mean, I had

no idea. Nothing. Three months ago! I just had Linda. . . . He'd go off every morning. Sometimes they let you use your old office to get another position. . . . I mean, I knew it was unusual that he was able to get away for this whole month, but all he said was—his words— he had 'earned it.' I had no idea—now I know what he meant. I just can't . . ." Her voice trailed away. She seemed to fold into herself. Then she whispered, as much to herself as to Maggie, "How could I have been so stupid!"

"Joanna, what did he mean about being worth more dead?"

Joanna wrapped her arms around her chest and thought for a while. "I'm not sure . . . but . . ." She turned away from Maggie.

"What?" Maggie pressed.

"If . . . if he were to die . . . before they—his company, the people he worked for—stopped paying insurance premiums, well . . . he . . . me, I suppose, would get . . . money." She closed her eyes.

"Is *that* why he's not taking the medicine?" Maggie asked.

"Maggie, I can't be sure. . . ." Suddenly, Joanna turned back to Maggie. "Was there . . . more?"

"Joanna . . ."

"Maggie, I have to know."

Maggie squeezed her hands. "He said . . . his . . . marriage . . . to you . . . was a mistake."

"He said that to you?"

Maggie nodded.

Joanna pressed a hand over her face.

"I said you loved him."

"I do."

"I think it made him madder."

Joanna shook her head.

"And then, when I said *I* loved him, he really blew up and said . . . more awful things."

"What?"

Maggie repeated what her father had said about her choosing to be with her mother. As she told it her tears began to flow again.

"He can be vicious when he wants to," Joanna said softly. "But that's not true what he said."

"But I did tell a judge I wanted to live with my mother."

"Maggie, how old were you?"

"Six."

"What else could he have expected?" Joanna said bitterly. "Look how much time he spends with Linda. Was it more with you? I doubt it. Oh, he's so self-centered!" She walked over to where Linda slept and stared down at her.

"Joanna . . ."

"What?"

"Where do you think he's gone?" Maggie asked.

"I don't know," Joanna said wearily. Then she

shrugged. "Apparently I know very little."

"Do you think he'll come back?"

Joanna did not answer right away. When she did she simply said, "I hope so." Then, with a crooked smile, she added, "We don't even have a car. We're marooned." She pursed her lips as if to keep from saying things.

Maggie gazed at Joanna. There appeared to be dark rings around her eyes. And for the first time she realized that Joanna bit her nails.

"I guess I shouldn't have said anything," Maggie said.

Joanna shook her head. "No, don't go blaming yourself. The fact is, I should have been the one who said something to him. About the medicine. It was wrong of me to ask you." She grimaced. "The truth is, I'm scared of him."

"You are?"

"Yes." She shrugged, adding, "I'm sorry."

The thought, "Everybody says they are sorry," flashed through Maggie's mind. Then she asked, "Is it losing his job that did all this?"

"God knows it would be enough," Joanna replied. "But there was Linda being born. And, just about the same time a doctor was telling him—in a way—that he was old. Then, on top of that, to be fired like that. Oh, *awful* people!" she cried. "Maggie, he put his heart into that business. Heart *and* soul. He loved it. More than anything. With all that coming apart . . .

"I didn't see it. I didn't. Any of it. I was too involved

with the baby. And myself." She shook her head sadly. "Oh, Maggie, what a rotten time for you!"

"Joanna . . . ?"

"What?"

"Is . . . is he going to . . . leave you?"

Maggie watched the play of emotions on Joanna's face. She could see sadness, tiredness, anger.

"I don't know," Joanna said finally.

"You could come live with us," Maggie offered.

Joanna threw back her head and laughed. "Your mother would love that!"

"No, really. I could ask her."

Joanna reached out and took Maggie's hand. "You are so dear. But you mustn't worry. He'll come back. We'll manage. I mean, we have to, don't we?"

"I guess."

Joanna gave a rueful smile. "You know, sometimes I forget how—I'm not putting you down—just the opposite—how young you are. Sometimes I really feel like we're . . . sisters."

Maggie smiled.

Joanna collected Maggie's dishes. "You must be exhausted. You should get to bed."

Maggie giggled. "Now you sound like a mother."

"Well," Joanna said, "you can take your pick: mother, sister, wife. I seem to be all of that. Or none," she added. "Anyway, maybe by the time you get up and go watch your bird he'll be back."

Maggie stared at her. "Did you know I was doing that?"

"Maggie, this is a very small place. Now, give us a hug and a kiss—I think we both need it. Then off to bed. Me, too."

They hugged each other for a long time.

"I really love you," Joanna said.

"I love you, too," Maggie replied. It was the first time she had ever said that to Joanna.

Maggie lay in her bed, staring up at the sky through her skylight. In spite of all that had happened, the one thing that kept coming back to her mind was the knowledge that her father, Joanna, even Tucker—all of them—knew she was watching the heron.

She kept telling herself that was the least important of all. Then why did it keep sneaking into her thoughts? A new notion came to her: Could it be *because* she was watching the heron that all of this had happened?

Even as she drifted off to sleep, she recalled what her father had said about the heron, that it used to be considered an omen, but that you had to choose which omen. Life. Or death.

Or was it, Maggie suddenly asked herself, was it the heron who chooses?

CHAPTER

27

The phone rang at three-thirty in the morning. At first Maggie thought it was her alarm telling her it was time to see the heron. The next moment she realized what it might be. When she did, she sat bolt upright, completely awake.

She scrambled to the loft door, popped it open, and looked down. Joanna had already switched on a lamp and reached the phone.

"Yes," she was saying, "this is Mrs. Lavchek."

As Maggie gazed from above there was a moment of silence. Then she heard Joanna moan slightly, and whisper, "Oh my God. . . ."

Heart thudding, Maggie scampered down the ladder.

"What's his condition now?" she heard Joanna ask.

Then, as if in answer to a question, "Yes, he's had a heart problem." Finally, "Where did you say he is?"

Maggie came to Joanna's side. Joanna reached out and took her hand. Joanna's hand was icy cold. As Maggie stood looking up at Joanna, trying to read the message on her face, Linda began to cry. A slight motion by Joanna sent Maggie hurrying over to the cradle. She picked the baby up. "Shhhh!" she whispered. "Shhhh!"

"I don't have another car," Joanna said into the phone. "This is just a summer rental for us and I don't know anyone here. Is there any way you can send someone?"

Maggie continued to utter soothing sounds to the baby but they did not work. She turned to Joanna with a look of appeal. Joanna held out an arm. Maggie brought Linda to her.

"No," Joanna said as she scooped the baby up and placed her over a shoulder. "And I have a four-month-old infant. Let me give you directions from Fall River to where I am." She gave them, thanked the person who had called her, and hung up.

"What happened?" Maggie asked.

Joanna did not answer. Instead she went over to her bed, sat down, and began to nurse Linda.

Maggie, her heart beating fast, watched anxiously. Joanna was staring down at the baby.

"Joanna . . ." Maggie pleaded softly.

Joanna looked up. Her jaw seemed slack. Her eyes were wide, and there was something wild in them. But they were dry. "Alan was in an accident," she said, her voice shaky. "Between here and Fall River. It must have happened shortly after he left you. It took a long time for them to track me down here. He only had Boston papers on him."

"Is he—all right?"

"No."

Maggie caught her breath. "What . . . ?"

"He's in serious—'not critical,' she said—condition. They think he had a heart attack while driving. The car went off the road. Flipped over."

The image of it and him brought Maggie a searing pain that twisted through her whole body. Her throat burned. She found it hard to breathe.

Joanna held out a hand. Maggie went forward and took it, then allowed herself to be included in Joanna's embrace. Linda continued nursing with small, wet sucking sounds.

Maggie pulled back. "Are they going to come get you?"

"They'll try."

"What . . . do you want me to do?"

"I don't know. I'm trying to think."

"Should I call my mom?"

"Not yet."

"I shouldn't have said any—"

"Maggie!" Joanna snapped, almost angrily.

"What?"

"Look at me!"

Startled, Maggie looked up. Though Joanna was crying, she said, "Now, listen to me, hard. Are you?"

"Yes."

"This is not your fault."

"But . . ."

"Don't even *allow* yourself to think it. You mustn't. This is *not* your fault. This is your father's *own* doing. Do you understand?"

Maggie swallowed, then nodded. "Okay," she said.

The phone rang.

"Get it," Joanna said, pushing Maggie gently.

Maggie scrambled across the room. "Hello?" she said.

"This is Fall River Memorial Hospital. May I speak to Mrs. Lavchek, please?"

"It's the hospital," Maggie whispered across the room.

"Take the message," Joanna called from across the room.

"She's nursing the baby," Maggie said. "Can I take a message? I'm Mr. Lavchek's daughter."

"Oh. Please tell your mother we're sending a security guard out to your place. We'll be there within forty-five minutes. Your mom should be waiting on the main road. It'll be too easy to miss that dirt road she told me about."

"Just a minute." Maggie relayed the message.

"Tell them fine," Joanna said. "Ask them if you can come, too."

Maggie took up the phone again. "She said fine. And she wants to know if I can come, too."

"How old are you?"

"Almost thirteen."

"Well," the woman on the phone said, "I think it would be best if—for this time, right now—if just your mother came. Tell her to please be ready."

"Okay." Maggie hung up the phone. "She said you should come without me."

"Okay. . . ."

"Are you going to take Linda?"

Joanna thought for a moment. "I better. No saying when I'll get back."

Maggie stared at her.

"Maggie, he'll be all right," Joanna said from across the room. "He will."

Maggie nodded automatically.

"Will you change Linda while I get some things together?" Joanna said, her voice growing firmer.

"Okay."

Maggie did as she was asked while Joanna rushed about stuffing a bag full of extra diapers and clothes for Linda. With Maggie holding the flashlight, they set off down the dirt road.

"Go back to sleep on the couch," Joanna instructed her. "I'll call you the first moment I can after seeing him. Are you going to be all right?"

"Yes. Don't worry."

"Maggie, I hate leaving you. Maybe I should have insisted. Or you could just come and wait in the waiting room or something. . . ."

"I'll be okay here."

"I've already decided to rent a car," Joanna went on. "I'll drive it back. We can't be here without a car."

The necessary decisions made, they walked in silence, following the ball of light that seemed to keep bouncing just out of reach in front of them. Now and again Maggie looked overhead, but it was too dark to see anything. Now and again she glanced up at Joanna.

Joanna had Linda tucked high on her shoulder. But she did not seem to be looking where she was going. Instead, with eyes staring before her, she marched forward mechanically.

"What will you do?" Maggie asked her.

"Now?"

"No . . . later."

Joanna remained silent for a while. "I don't know," she said. "Let's see how bad he is. Maggie, I have no idea what money there is, or about insurance, or . . ." Despair had crept into her voice. "Anything. I was thinking I should call his office, but I don't know if he's cut off all contact with it. He's kept all this stuff to himself. I'm appalled. I mean, I know *nothing*. I just never thought . . ." She stopped talking.

They reached the main road. It stretched to the right and to the left, a dark, dead river. A car swept by, its lights momentarily blinding them.

"Should I go back to Seattle?" Maggie asked.

"We'll talk it through when I get back. I'll have a better

sense of things. It might be helpful if you stayed. Maybe not. We'll see. Anyway, we'll work it out together. Do what's best."

"Joanna . . ."

"What?"

Maggie took a breath and then said, "I love Dad. But I like you more."

Joanna looked at her, briefly rested a hand on Maggie's shoulder, squeezed it gently, then turned away.

The car from the hospital swooped down on them. A young man in a uniform jumped out of the car. "Mrs. Lavchek?"

"That's me."

"Get on in then."

Joanna slid into the car. Maggie shut the door behind her. "Soon as I can I'll call," Joanna promised.

"Don't worry," Maggie said.

CHAPTER

28

The car taking Joanna and Linda to the hospital made a sharp U-turn, then sped away. Maggie watched it until it was completely gone, its red taillights fading like dying embers. Holding the flashlight before her, she set off down the dirt road.

It had been dark on the main road but on the dirt road, with trees on either side and above, it was darker yet. After a few yards Maggie halted and listened to her own heart beating. She looked back and could made out where the dirt road met the main road, a semicircle of gray on black. She moved the flashlight about, probing the edges of the night with the yellow beam. "My sword of light," she told herself. "It shall protect me."

As the crickets filled the air with their busy noise, she

decided they were counting to infinity but were too stupid to know they'd never reach it. And when she heard a rustle from somewhere in the woods, she made up her mind it was that rabbit again. He had come with his entire family to see her walk by.

The image of the rabbit family made her smile and she began to walk more quickly, occasionally scuffing the dirt or rocks with her feet. She knew she was acting brave and it pleased her. But when she saw the cabin lights ahead she began to run, quickly covering the last few yards.

The door banged behind her. As small and crowded as the cabin was it seemed very empty. Baby smells filled the air and reminded her who was not there.

For a moment Maggie thought of Linda, her half sister. She had thought the baby was going to be the most important part of this trip. But Linda had turned out to be the least important. For her, Maggie, anyway. Not Joanna.

The couch bed was all a-tumble. Maggie went to the fridge and took an apple, sat on the bed, and began to munch it. Suddenly she sensed how alone she was and felt a great desire to call her mother. But when she looked at the clock over the stove—not even five o'clock—and calculated the time it was in Seattle—three hours earlier—she decided against it. It was the realization that she could not call that broke through her last resistance. She flung herself down on the couch bed, pressed her face into a pillow, and began to cry very softly.

She was asleep when the phone rang. All the same she was up in an instant and grabbed the receiver off the hook.

"Hello?"

"Maggie, hi." It was Joanna.

"Is he all right?"

"Yes and no."

"What do you mean?"

"He did have a heart attack. Lost control of the car. It went off the road and flipped. When the car went over he broke an arm and a couple of ribs. He also has terrible black eyes and all kinds of bruises. The key question is about internal injuries. They can't be sure about that yet. It could—believe it or not—have been much worse. At least so far. But depending on what else, well . . . he might . . . it's possible, he might . . . not make it."

"Did you talk to him?"

"Not really. He's got all this medication, and tubes stuck in . . . not pretty. But he's alive. And I held his hand. It was warm."

Maggie felt sick.

"I'm trying to work through arrangements. It's total confusion. There are questions as to whether he's even covered by medical insurance or not. Has to do with when he left his job. I'm trying to find out if that part ended or not. A mess," she said. "A real mess. But it's still early."

"What time is it?"

"About six-thirty. Soon as I can get a car I'll get back. How you doing?"

"Okay."

"Sure?"

"Yes."

"Maybe you should call your mother. Just so she knows."

"It's too early there."

"I suppose. You sure you're going to be all right?"

"I'm okay."

"Bless you. If I get hung up I'll call again."

"All right."

"Maggie?"

"What?"

"Now listen: Your father—and I—made this mess. You didn't."

"Okay."

"And I love you."

"I love you."

Maggie hung up the phone but stood for a while looking out at the lawn, at the lake. It looked the way it always did. But it felt different.

She made up the couch bed, then folded it up. Afterward she climbed into her loft and got dressed, then came back down.

It was while drinking a glass of juice that she suddenly remembered the heron. Tucker might be out there on his island, waiting to kill it. She began to run to the marsh.

CHAPTER

29

It was something of a shock for Maggie to see that nothing had changed on the marsh. Though no heron was in sight, it was all perfectly normal. The water surface lay unperturbed. The green polka-dot lilies floated easily. The dragonflies darted about as though threading unseen needles in the air. What had happened to her father appeared unconnected.

Sitting on her rock, knees drawn up, Maggie could see nothing to indicate that Tucker was on the island. She decided he was not there.

The more she sat, the calmer she became. Slowly now, with care, she went over what had happened between her father and herself, deciding that it had not been an argument. All she had done was try and warn him about not taking his medicine. She knew she had been in the right.

For a moment resentment flared against Joanna for her request that she be the one to speak to her father. Joanna, Maggie told herself, should have spoken to him herself. Then, with a sigh, Maggie reminded herself about what she knew now, that Joanna and her father were not getting along, that her father had been keeping secret most of what was happening to him. And Maggie could see now that Joanna was being bullied by her father. Hadn't she even said she was scared of him? *That* was almost the worst part.

Still, in her heart, Maggie wished that she herself had said nothing. And she never should have called him stupid, though—she could hear herself saying it—not taking your medicine *was* stupid.

She wondered what would happen to her father and Joanna now. If he lived. The thought made her cringe.

One thing was clear: This time together at the lake would not be repeated. Whatever happened to them, together or individually, things would be altered. Joanna would have to. . . . What would Joanna have to do? She would have to stop being scared. And her father would no longer be able to manage everything.

Into Maggie's head popped the answer to a question she'd asked herself when she first came to the lake. It was when she had tried to recall when and where she had received the Merlin the Magician doll. Now she remembered: It had been a gift from her father, a kind of good-bye gift that he'd given her the day he left their home, the day he separated from her mother.

"That's me," he told her, when she had opened up the box. "Merlin the Magician. Call me whenever you have a problem. I'll fix it like magic." And he had snapped his fingers. Maggie sighed: It had been the wrong kind of magic.

Maggie closed her eyes, opened them, and stared at a distant place in the marsh. Then she turned back to the area in front of her. The heron was there.

Maggie caught her breath. The bird seemed more beautiful than ever before.

"Do you know what happened?" Maggie said to the bird. She spoke evenly, her voice low but firm.

For a moment the bird seemed to pause in its search for food as if it had heard her words. Other than that, it gave no indication that it was aware of Maggie's presence. Encouraged nonetheless, Maggie related everything that had happened. When she finished her tale, she grew thoughtful for a while. Then she said, "There's something else. Can I tell you? I never told anyone. Not even my mother."

She waited a moment. She knew exactly what she wanted to say—had said it in her mind many times—but found it difficult to speak the words out loud. Then she said, "The people I love—sometimes—I don't like them."

She waited for something to happen. Nothing did.

With a sense of relief, Maggie sighed. She gazed at the bird and her heart swelled with gratitude. Then she laughed. "But, you know what? If you let something happen to you, I'll dislike you, too."

It was after sitting for a while more that it occurred to Maggie that she should go back to the cabin and stay by the phone just in case Joanna called. Joanna might worry if she were not there. And maybe it was time to call her mother. She speculated as to how her mother would react to the news. Reluctantly, she stood up.

"I'm leaving," she called out to the heron.

That time the bird lifted its head and looked right at her.

"When you look at me," Maggie asked it, "what do you see? Or think?"

The bird did not move. Just stared. Maggie began to feel uneasy. "Are you trying to tell me something? Was it about what I said?" She was tense now, absolutely certain the heron was trying to send her a message.

"Is something else going to happen?" she asked. The bird continued to gaze at her.

Trying to push away the feelings of dread that were engulfing her, Maggie took a few tentative steps in the direction of the cabin. She stopped, afraid to leave. *If something happens to the bird, my father will die.* The thought—as clear as if a voice had spoken into her ear—held her fast.

She turned around and moved back toward the marsh.

The heron—at its favorite feeding spot by the island—snapped its head down and brought up a tiny fish.

Maggie stepped to the marsh edge. Once there, she eased off her sneakers and stepped carefully into the water. It was almost warm. "I'm not going to hurt you," she announced. The bird lifted its head and looked at her.

Maggie took another step forward. This time she sank into the soft bottom. Almost losing her footing, she swayed precariously.

"I'm okay," Maggie said softly, and took another step forward. The bird continued to watch her. Maggie, returning the look, suddenly knew what she wanted to do, had to do. She would touch the bird. If she could touch it, all would be well, because touching the magic meant you and the magic became one.

"Would you let me?" Maggie asked, as if the bird already knew what she was thinking and could answer. But the heron only stared fixedly at her.

As Maggie began to move forward, her heart beat furiously. She had the sensation that she was moving the way the heron did, contemplating each movement, each part of each movement. Her eyes were on the bird and nothing else. She lost all sense of time. And always, she kept one hand extended before her, fingers loose, shivering gently like an undulating fan.

Gradually the distance between them decreased. The heron, as if transfixed, held its place, its eyes staring right at Maggie. Maggie could see now that the bird's colors were much more complex than she had seen from the shore. There were shades of grays, blues, blacks. Even the whites had many shades. She began to see individual feathers, how they were layered, how coarse some were, while others were fine and small. And though the bird was standing still, the tips of some feathers fanned and flowed, ruffling in a breeze that Maggie could not feel.

"Please, please," Maggie pleaded softly. "Please let me touch you."

There seemed to be no sound but the beating of her heart, no sense of motion that was movement. Instead there was an unfolding that brought her closer and closer. And as she drew nearer and nearer, the heron continued to gaze at her with its unblinking lemon eyes.

There were but twenty inches now from the tip of Maggie's fingers to the heron's crown. Every part of her body seemed to be tingling. It would take two more steps. One more step. Maggie held her breath. Then, as slowly as she had ever done anything in her life, she shifted her right foot up, heard the slight sucking sound as it pulled against the bottom mud, moved it forward even as she stretched as far as possible, her arm and fingers quivering . . . and gently—hardly more than a breath of finger to feather—she touched the heron on the side of its head and sensed the silky down of the tiny feathers, its warmth, its life.

The bird blinked and slowly coiled back its head. Then it turned and without any movement of panic or sound of alarm, rose up out of the water into the air. With its great wings flapping, it flew away.

Maggie, her heart pounding, and not knowing whether to laugh or cry, watched it go. Only gradually did she become aware that she was shaking. What she needed to do was get on solid land.

She looked about. The island was the nearest place. She headed for that and reached it in moments, clambering up on the bank. Once there she let out a slow breath. She was no longer shaking but she did feel exhausted.

Gradually, she edged about the island until she found Tucker's passageway. First she sat on the bank and scraped mud off her legs. Once that was done, she got on hands and knees and crawled to the interior of the island. There, in the cocoonlike cave of bushes, she lay down.

As she relived what she had done, her eyes grew heavy. Dreamy. The more she thought about it, the more extraordinary she knew it was. Would anyone— she asked herself—believe it?

30

"What are you doing here?" came the voice.

Maggie opened her eyes and found herself staring into Tucker's face. She sat up quickly.

"This is my place," he said.

"I fell asleep," Maggie replied.

"I know, nut. I just want to know how come you're here."

"What time is it?"

"I don't know. After eight. Did you wade out here?"

"Yes."

"You are so weird," he said. "I wouldn't walk on that bottom. Nothing but muck. Tracks up everything."

"Why did you come?" she suddenly asked, looking around for the bow and arrows.

"I always come here."

"Why?"

"I told you, dummy, it's my place." Then he grinned at her.

"Were you going to kill the heron?"

"Do you think I would?"

"Yes."

"Then you're right."

She stared at him. "Do you know why?" she asked.

" 'Course I do."

"Well, tell me."

He studied her silently, then turned away. "Anyone ever say you ask too many questions?"

"No."

"Well, you do."

Suddenly Maggie knew that though he might kill the bird, she was sure he did not know why he would do it.

"Why don't you get out now?" Tucker said, gesturing toward the passageway with a thumb.

"My father was almost killed," she blurted out.

"What?"

"Last night."

"What do you mean?"

"He was in a car accident."

"No kidding?"

Maggie nodded.

"Smashup?" Tucker drew his hands together with a smack.

Maggie winced, but nodded and said, "He was driving. And . . . and he had a heart attack. I guess he lost control of the car."

Tucker was all attention now. "The car flip over?" he asked. Maggie sensed he really wanted to know.

"Yes."

"What happened to him?"

That time it was Maggie who looked away. "He was hurt badly."

Tucker plucked at her arm. "Like what? Breaking bones, stuff like that?"

Maggie felt sick. But she nodded and told Tucker what Joanna had told her.

"Is he going to die?" Tucker asked, his voice a little more subdued than before.

"Maybe."

"Oh. That would never happen to my father or mother," Tucker insisted. "They're so careful. You know, my sister dying . . ."

Maggie watched him carefully. "Would you want it to happen?"

"What?"

"Your parents . . . ?"

"No, not really," Tucker answered. He was looking down at something on the ground. Then he looked up. "Then—if your father almost got killed—how come you're here?"

"My stepmother is at the hospital."

"That the woman I saw you with at church?"

"Yes."

"I thought she was your sister!"

"My stepmother. She had to go to the hospital but I wasn't going to be allowed in."

"Yeah. They always think kids mess around." He studied the ground again. "You could have come over to my place."

"I did."

He looked at her, puzzled. "What do you mean?"

"I came here."

Tucker stared at her. Then he grinned. "Right. You got it. This *is* my place. I'll tell you something: My parents don't even know about it. You're the only one. But if they found out . . ." He shook his head. "They're always after me, you know, about doing things *right*. They get so weird about that."

"I saw your father hit you in church."

Tucker hung his head. "Yeah. I was fooling around. Trying to get you to laugh. So it was right what he did."

"Why?"

He shrugged. "He keeps me good. It isn't easy." He grinned. "I'm always doing things."

"Like what?"

"Look, Big Bird, I just don't want anyone around here. Anyone! I mean, until you came around in that cabin there was hardly *anyone* here. Weekends, maybe. That's all. So this is mine. But it's all right, *your* being here I mean, what with your father almost getting killed and all. And then, anyway, you don't live here, do you? Seattle, right? That's about three thousand miles away."

"How do you know?"

"I looked it up in the map book."

"Something else happened this morning," Maggie said.

"What?"

"I . . . touched the blue heron."

Tucker's eyes opened wide. "You did *what?*"

"Touched the heron."

"Get off. . . . They don't even let you get near them! You look in their direction. Zoom! Off they go. Try shooting them with a gun but you can't. They can tell. Off they go. Zam! Only way to get them is with a bow and arrow. You know why?"

Maggie shook her head.

"Because it's so sneaky."

"Tucker, I touched it."

"Did not!" he replied.

"I did!"

"Okay, how'd you do it?"

Maggie told him. And Tucker listened raptly as she related exactly how it had happened. When she was finished he was staring at her with admiration.

"Neat . . ." he said.

"*Please* don't tell anyone," she said.

"Why?"

"It's a secret."

"You told me."

"You're different. Anyway, I don't think anyone would believe me."

"I believe you. Man, I couldn't be that patient."

"Tucker . . . if you watched it, and studied it, you could."

"Not me. I'd mess up. I always do."

"Maybe you wouldn't."

He was looking down. "Yeah . . ." he said, "I would."

After a moment Maggie said, "Tucker?"

"What?"

"I think—in a couple of days—I'll have to go home. To Seattle." She took a deep breath, then said, "Tucker . . ."

He looked up at her.

"Please—*please*—don't kill the heron. I love it . . . so much."

"Love . . . that's girl stuff."

"It's not!"

"Well—I don't know. . . ."

Very slowly Maggie reached out her hand. Tucker started and drew back. But Maggie continued to move her hand forward slowly. This time Tucker did not move but just stared at her until she touched fingers to his cheek.

"Please . . ." Maggie said. *"Please."*

CHAPTER

31

"*Now Margaret—*" the nurse said as they walked down the hospital corridor. "That's your name, right?"

"Maggie."

"Maggie, I'm counting on you not to stay for more than a few moments. *Five* minutes, to be exact."

Maggie was trying hard not to look at the other patients, each of them in bathrobes or green hospital shifts. Some were just sitting. Others were trying to walk with the aid of walkers. One man was pushing a contraption to which he was connected by a lot of tubes. All looked sad and slow.

"I know you want to be with your dad," the nurse continued. "But the best way you can help him is to be cheerful, tell him things are fine at home and that you love him a whole lot. But all that's true anyway, I'm sure."

"Sort of . . ." Maggie murmured.

"Make sure you tell him they are. Now, here he is."

Maggie looked at the door. The name "Alan Lavchek" was written in black letters on the door.

"Now remember what I told you. He still has those black eyes. He's got a tube in his nose, plus other tubes feeding him through an arm. I just don't want you shocked or anything. Okay?"

Maggie nodded.

"And believe me, Maggie, he's a lot better than when he came in. Lord, what drinking does!"

"He *wasn't* drinking," Maggie said firmly. "He had a heart attack."

"Well, anyway, he's not out of harm's way yet."

"I know."

"I'll be right out here. After five minutes I'll have to come in if you don't come out. Now be a good girl." She gave Maggie a little pat and a push.

Maggie, trying not to show her nervousness, twisted the door handle and stepped into the small room. The light was low, and it took a moment for her eyes to adjust to the gloominess. Gradually she made out the bed on which her father lay. The black eyes, the tubes, an arm in a sling—she saw it all, just as she had been told and warned. It was still a shock.

She went up to the bed and stood near. His eyes were closed.

"Dad . . . ?" Maggie whispered, even as she slipped her hand into his one free one. "It's me, Maggie."

After a moment her father shifted his head, flickered his eyes open, and squeezed her hand. "Hello, kid," he said. His voice was weak and breathy.

"Hi."

After a moment he said, "Sight for sore eyes. Dumb joke."

"I'm . . . glad to see you."

"I bet."

For a moment neither spoke. Maggie, feeling the tears well up in her eyes, said, "Dad . . . I'm sorry I called you . . . stupid."

He made a tiny shake of his head. "You were right. And . . . this is nothing you did. I . . . messed up our time together, that's all."

"No . . ."

"And a lot more besides."

"Things will get better."

"Maybe."

"They will." In the silence that followed, Maggie struggled to find something to say. "Is it all right here?" she asked, embarrassed at the stupidity of the question.

Mr. Lavchek grimaced. "I like the cabin more. Joanna . . . Joanna says . . . you've been great."

"I called my mother. I'm going back to Seattle tomorrow morning."

Her father said nothing. Then he said, "I'll miss you."

"I'll miss you."

"Call me like you used to, kid. Even if I'm here."

"I will."

"I screwed up your birthday, too."

"Dad, that doesn't matter!"

"Screwed up everything."

"I just want you to get better," Maggie whispered, fighting back the tears.

"Okay."

"Dad . . . ?"

"What?"

"Joanna really loves you."

"I know."

"And so does Linda."

"Who?"

"Linda."

"She's not so nice as you are."

"And I love you, too."

"You're the best."

"I have to go," Maggie said. She bent over and kissed her father's cheek. It was in need of a shave. She straightened up and made a tentative gesture to move away. He clung to her hand briefly, feebly. There were tears trickling down his cheeks.

"I'll call you a lot," Maggie said.

"Maggie?"

"What?"

"Forget the magic. It doesn't work."

Gently, Maggie took away her hand. She reached the door just as the nurse was opening it. "Good girl," the nurse said.

Maggie hated her.

CHAPTER

32

Joanna and Linda were waiting in the front lobby.

"Should we go right home?" Joanna said.

Maggie, afraid to talk lest she burst into tears, simply nodded.

"Not good, is it?" Joanna said.

Maggie agreed with a movement of her head.

During the drive to the cabin neither spoke. Maggie wanted to think about her father. But no matter how hard she tried, her thoughts kept slipping off to the heron. And Tucker. She had not seen him since their time together on the island. In all the confusion, the comings and goings that had to do with her father, there had been no time. Two days ago she had canoed to his house. He was not there. She did leave a note saying she was going home in two days and wanted to talk to him. Whether he got the note or not, whether he had tried to see her, whether he was avoiding her, waiting until she left, she knew none of that. It worried her a lot.

When they pulled up to the cabin, she and Joanna remained seated in the car.

"Joanna?"

"Hmm?"

"What are you going to do?" Maggie asked.

Joanna gave something of a sigh. "Pack up. Get back to Boston. It's too difficult and isolated here for me and the baby. And then . . . we'll see. For one thing, I'll have to find a job. The what, the where, the how, I'm just not sure."

"I could have stayed longer."

Joanna patted Maggie's hand. "It's lovely of you to offer, but we have to work things out without you. Still, you never know," she said with a rueful smile, "we may all turn up on your doorstep in Seattle. Anyway, you're going to give me a hand with the packing and that's a big help."

When Joanna made no move to get out of the car, Maggie was sure she had something else to say.

"Can I ask you something?" Joanna finally said.

"Sure."

"What is it that gets you up in the mornings to look at that bird?"

Maggie tried to think how to put her thoughts into words but gave up. Instead she said, "I think you have to see for yourself. Would you like to? It's there most times."

"Only if you want me to."

Maggie thought for a moment. She could hear herself saying that she should not, that it was important that she keep the heron just for herself and Tucker. "Would you mind very much—be insulted—if we didn't?"

Joanna gave a wan smile. "More secrets?"

"No," Maggie protested, feeling her cheeks burn. "It's just that . . . well, it's not *always* there. Or it might not come if . . . anyone else came." She was struggling to say what she really felt. "I mean, it's just that it's sort of . . ." She could not say the word.

"Private?" Joanna suggested.

"I guess."

"I'm not insulted."

Maggie sighed. "I wish you were my sister," she said.

"Bless you," Joanna returned.

CHAPTER

33

The alarm under Maggie's pillow rang at six-thirty. But she was already awake and dressed. For just a moment she lay back on the bed, staring up into the sky, then at the crystal that hung above her head. The little loft danced with rainbows.

She reached up and put it into her pocket, then climbed down the loft ladder. Her suitcase and duffel bag were already packed and waiting. The cabin itself looked unusually neat, even bare.

Joanna was up, too, nursing the baby. "Go on now," she said. "Don't be too long. I'm glad you're getting breakfast on the plane."

Maggie hurried outside. It was already warm. And there was no mist. Such sun as there was cast long shadows. She moved down the path, wanting to run but restraining herself. Even so she was at the edge of the marsh in a matter of moments. One quick survey and she knew the heron was not there.

Her heart sank.

Still, determined to wait for as long as time allowed, Maggie climbed onto her rock, drew her knees up, clasped them, and stared vacantly before her.

She was upset and growing more upset by the moment. She really had thought she'd gotten through to Tucker. Maybe she had. More likely not. Either way, she would never know. It was the not knowing that was so unbearable.

Her foot slipped and she had to adjust her position. That was when she saw, partially buried in leaves at the side of the rock, the bow and arrows. For a moment, she stared at them, hardly believing what she was seeing. Then, in a mad rush, she climbed down and picked them up. The bow had its string cut. The arrows had been broken in two.

For a moment she held the bits in her hand, until, with a surge of joy, she flung them into the woods. Then she swung about to face the island and stared at it. Bursting into movement, she whipped off shoes, socks, and jeans, grabbed her crystal, and plunged into the water. She did not care how much noise she made nor how wet she became. Once, twice—she was going fast—she stumbled, becoming soaked to the waist. She did not care.

When she reached the island she scrambled up, then edged around to Tucker's passageway. Once there, she slipped the loop that held the crystal onto the branch of a bush. It dangled right over the entrance to the path. There was no way Tucker would miss it.

"Maggie!" She heard Joanna call. "We have to leave."

Maggie all but jumped back down into the water and waded back to shore. Once there, she scraped away some of the mud, picked up her shoes and clothing, and began to hurry up the path. She'd change in the car. But with a sudden wrench, she made herself stop and turned to take one more look. She gasped. The heron was there.

As always it was standing still, gazing into the water. Then, even as Maggie watched, it began to move, move ever so slowly, paying no attention to her at all. Even so, just to look at it made Maggie's heart swell.

"I'll never hate you!" she called. "Never!" And turning, she ran back to the waiting car.

Tucker sat on Maggie's rock looking out over the marsh. Some twenty-five feet before him was the heron. For a long while Tucker just sat there and watched. Then, slowly, he dug into a pocket and pulled out the crystal Maggie had left him. Holding it up he let it dangle in the air. Rainbows danced about the marsh. "Hello," Tucker said softly to the bird. "You see this? Well, I'm Maggie's friend."